The Secret Mage

The Secret Mage

Elice, the Great (Book One)

Jennifer Roachford

Curly Tales Publishing

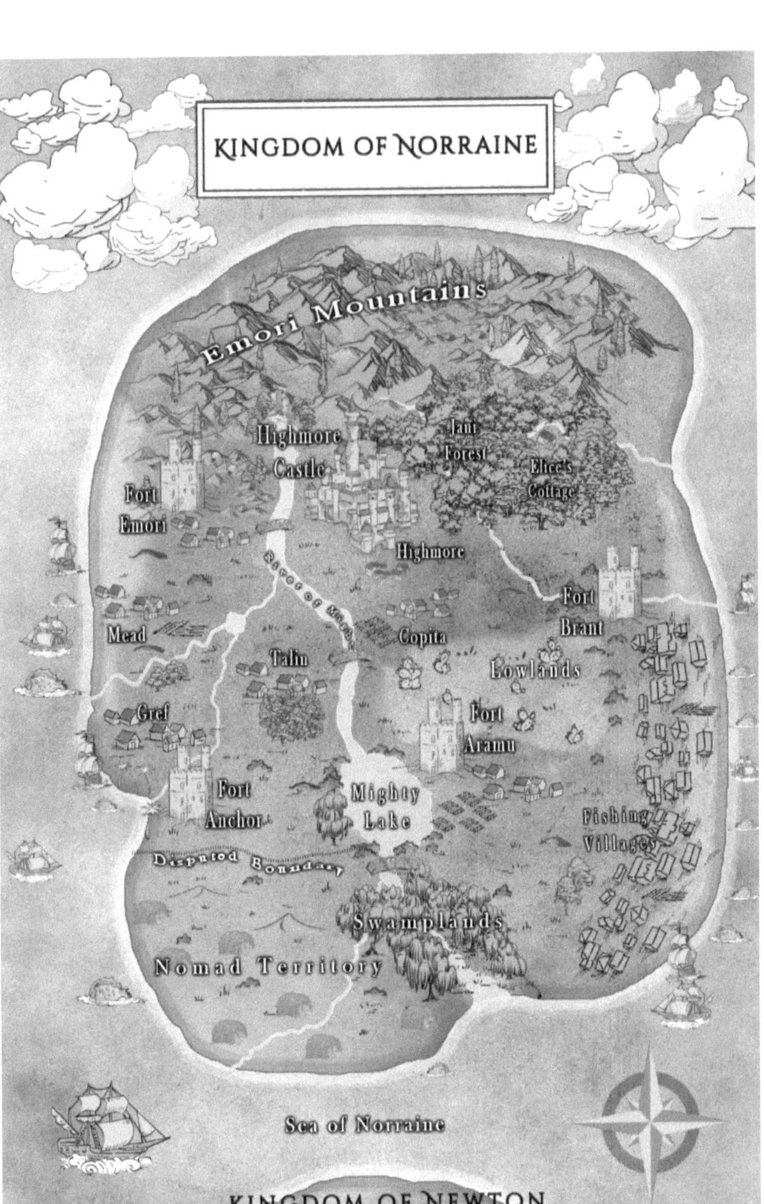

KINGDOM OF NORRAINE
Emori Mountains
Highmore Castle
Iani Forest
Elice's Cottage
Fort Emori
Highmore
Fort Brant
Mead
River of Mira
Copita
Talu
Lowlands
Gref
Fort Aramu
Fort Anchor
Mighty Lake
Fishing Villages
Disputed Boundary
Swamplands
Nomad Territory
Sea of Norraine
KINGDOM OF NEWTON

One

A tiny storm grew in her palm. Thin wisps of wind mixed with water molecules in her hands to create a miniature cyclone. Elice sat cross-legged on the hardwood floor in front of her couch with her wide eyes fixated on her newest creation. Finally, after weeks of sneaking around to practice, she found the perfect balance of air and water.

The low thud of Lenore's walking cane echoed throughout the cottage. Elice gasped and released her spell. The water and air stopped spinning around each other. As they separated, the air brushed past her hip-length curly hair while the water fell and splashed on the floor.

Lenore appeared in the doorway to the living room. Elice glanced in her direction, knowing all too well that Lenore wore her usual scowl on her wrinkled face. She wondered if Lenore saw her using magic. Elice wasn't a seer like Lenore, and reading facial expressions on the aged woman was near impossible since she always had the same scrunched-up look of disgust on her features.

"Girl," Lenore called out. "Grab my traveling bag." Her gray hair hung like flat strips from her head, barely long enough to reach the top of the silver necklace she wore over her floor-length brown frock.

With a wrinkled hand, Lenore adjusted the talisman that swung from the end of the chain and gripped her wooden walking cane with her other hand. Without another glance, the woman hobbled over to the small circular table in the corner of the room and carefully lowered herself onto one of the two wooden chairs.

Elice stood from her spot beside the old couch. They rarely sat on it, and time had taken its toll on the structure and fabric. It looked like it would crumble with the slightest touch. She spent most of her time sitting on the floor, anyway—closer to the ground where she could be closer to the earth. Having control of three of the four elements meant she had an acute awareness of nature and its properties.

She walked toward the bookshelf near the couch, her dark curls bouncing with every step, and grabbed Lenore's bag from the floor. She hesitated when she turned and saw the woman dozing off, her head lolling down to her chest. Slowly, Elice walked past the withered couch and her sleeping cot along the opposite wall.

"Lenore," she whispered, afraid to startle the woman as she slept.

Lenore's beady eyes snapped open with a start and narrowed in on Elice's face. She snatched her bag from Elice's hands and tossed it on the table to rummage through it.

Elice stood still for a moment as she watched Lenore dig through the contents of her bag. Lenore's wrinkled fingers pushed vials and other knickknacks around with a quivering hand.

Elice didn't like when Lenore made the long journey alone to the nearest town to sell or trade their homemade crafts and trinkets. Even though the money she would make allowed her to buy food or other things they needed, Elice knew how dangerous it was for the woman to travel by herself.

But Elice couldn't leave their meager cottage in the secluded clearing deep in the Jani Forest. She only knew of the world outside her home through books and stories Lenore would bring back from her travels.

It was better this way, Lenore always reminded her. Time and again, Lenore would tell her why she needed to stay in their home. She said Elice was better off sequestered from the world until she could learn to control her growing powers.

Even though Elice understood this, she continued to stare at Lenore, a hint of longing attached to the fear of her leaving again. Each time Lenore took off, Elice would beg to go with her. She would tell Lenore she was finally ready to enter the world, that she had enough control of her magic to make the journey without using her powers, and could be around other people for once. She would plead, promise, cry, and scream until Lenore simply put her foot down and told her no.

Then she would leave. And Elice would be alone again.

Lenore grabbed a sheet of paper she had placed to the side of their cramped table and passed it to Elice.

"Study," the woman said, her gravelly voice barely above a whisper.

Elice took the paper and returned to her usual seat on the floor. She forced herself to read from the list. It had several techniques she needed to work on during Lenore's absence. Many included calming methods she still hadn't mastered, such as mind blocking and envisioning strategies. Since the law required all mages to control their powers, she needed to learn to push them down before they forced their way out.

However, it proved to be a struggle to control it, and there weren't many books available in the middle of the forest for Elice to learn from. Besides, there weren't many people who were able to control more than one element, let alone three. She was in unchartered territory.

Elice looked up from her paper and bit her lip. She wanted to point out how tired the old woman looked, considering how frail and brittle her body was.

As Lenore closed her bag and stood from the table to begin her long trek through the forest, Elice simply said, "Have a safe trip."

Lenore grunted in response. "Keep your energy focused on your studies." She spoke over her shoulder, not bothering to turn around.

Elice sucked her bottom lip as Lenore shuffled her way to the door. Unable to hold it in any longer, Elice jumped up and took a few steps toward Lenore. "I still think you shouldn't go."

An extended silence rolled over them as Lenore stood still, anchored by her sturdy cane. Elice hesitated—the woman would get upset that Elice brought this up again, but she had to try. "At least," she continued, "not by yourself."

This caused Lenore to turn around, using her cane to help her body move in a circle. "You're not ready," she said in a slow, almost pained tone, her voice giving out on the last word.

"But I feel ready," Elice said, grabbing a fistful of her tattered and stained off-white dress. "And it's not safe for you to travel all that way alone. What if something happens to you?"

Lenore drew in a raspy breath. "But it's not safe for you to be out there, around all those people."

"I've been working so hard at controlling my magic. I think I'm finally ready to leave the cottage."

"No. You haven't mastered it yet."

"Don't you think I can master it better when I'm actually exposed to real-life situations?" Elice argued.

"Real-life situations? You can't even have a conversation without acting like a child and letting your emotions overpower you."

"I'm not acting like a child." Elice had to force her foot to stay still so she wouldn't stomp it on the ground.

"Look at you," said Lenore with a hoarse voice, pointing at Elice with her free hand. "You're pouting and yelling like a baby, and the air around you is as thick as fog."

Elice looked down at her hands, balled into fists. She loosened the grip on her frayed dress, and the moisture in the air dissipated. She hadn't even realized she was controlling the air and water around her to create the fog in the first place.

"You are not ready," said the old woman, turning and opening the door. She left without letting Elice say another word, shutting the door behind her.

Elice sighed as she stared at the closed door. Feeling defeated, she grabbed her checklist again and went back to work on her techniques, though she couldn't focus. Her mind wandered to the words Lenore had always told her.

"You are a danger to those around you," Lenore had always said. "You must concentrate on controlling your magic. Until then, you will stay in this cottage."

So Elice remained alone, attempting to suppress her innate powers, hoping Lenore would return in time for her birthday. The woman didn't mention it, and Elice knew better than to remind her. Like she had many other times before, she would likely spend her birthday alone, with no family or friends to celebrate with.

Two

The next day, Elice found herself in her usual spot on the floor. Her mini tornado spun into a two-inch tall structure in her hand. She knew she should practice her meditative breaths, but her heart swelled with pride whenever her storm grew bigger.

A bang at the door made Elice drop her spell. At first, she wondered why the sound came from the door. Lenore wouldn't be back for a few days—maybe even a week. Elice's eyes scanned the room, wondering if the source of the noise came from inside the house instead.

Nothing seemed out of place, so she raised her palm to begin a new spell. With Lenore gone, she was free to practice whatever and whenever she wanted. While Elice worried for the woman, she relished the chance to practice without Lenore sneaking up on her.

She called on the surrounding wind, her hand open to receive the light tickle from the air, when she heard the sound again. This time it was unmistakable—someone had knocked on the front door. The sound of four more heavy bangs made her jump. Her heart pounded as she stared at the wooden door. No one ever came to her house. She lived in the middle of the Jani Forest with Lenore for a reason.

She wondered if the person would go away if she ignored them. Then a terrible thought occurred to her. What if something happened to Lenore, and the person on the other side of the door was trying to bring her home? Her heart continued to race as she stood and inched her way to the door.

She paused with her hand on the knob. Lenore was the only person she ever had contact with, and she kept Elice in this secluded cottage because the king had outlawed magic many years ago. Elice shook her head and swallowed her fear. With a deep breath, she pulled the door open.

Then she froze.

She stared at the man before her, the light brown of his eyes reflecting the sunlight that filtered through the tall trees high above her cottage. He was a head taller and had brown skin like her own. He wore the uniform of a soldier—Elice recognized the King's Army emblem on his left lapel from a book on her shelf. The man stared at her too. Curiosity mixed with bewilderment on his puzzled face, and he opened his mouth to say something, but no words came out.

That's when Elice noticed a flash of light coming from around his neck. She followed the light to a silver chain around his neck, and something familiar glittered at the end. It was Lenore's talisman, the one she wore every day. It wasn't just any trinket, but the woman's protection stone—created by mages long before the ban on magic, and imbued with spells meant to protect the wearer from harm. The talisman never left Lenore's neck. Why did this man have it, and where was Lenore? Elice's eyes narrowed at the sight of this stranger wearing her guardian's protection charm.

He mumbled her name and reached his hand out. On instinct, she drew her hands up, gathering a gust of air. With her palms facing forward, she blasted the wind from her hands and forced the man back from her doorstep.

She only meant to push him, but the burst was so strong he flew a few feet in the air and landed on the hard ground behind him. Elice kept her hands in front of her body in case he stood and attacked her, but he didn't stir. She took a step closer, her curly hair blowing from the wind that continued to spiral around her.

With a calming breath, she lowered her fingers, and the wind settled with her. Still, she worried the man might get up at any moment. She took another step closer toward his feet, his boots covered in mud that stuck to the ridged soles. She hesitated before reaching out with one of her bare feet and nudging his shoe, but he continued to lie still.

At first, she wondered how he knew her name. Hearing it slip from his lips had made her react with such a strong force of air she thought she had killed him. She crouched closer and noticed the rise and fall of his chest. *Good, he's still alive*, she thought, until she realized this man might have harmed her guardian. How else would he have gotten the necklace the old woman wore every day?

Looking down once again at the unconscious man, she wondered if he had hurt Lenore and stole the talisman. Elice noticed his muscled form beneath his uniform, so he could easily overpower a frail old woman like Lenore.

Knowing she needed to get answers out of him, she straightened her back and raised her arms once more, her fingers spread wide. She focused on the ground beneath her bare feet and called upon the roots and vines that grew underneath. Out they came, breaking through the soil and twisting their way above ground to wrap around the soldier's wrists and ankles. Dozens of roots popped out and made shackles around his limbs, wrapping multiple times to hold him in place.

Elice kneeled beside him and gave the thick earthen handcuffs around his wrist a tug to make sure they were strong enough to hold him down. Satisfied with her work, she stood and began pacing the dirt floor, her mind reeling over what had happened. A noise from behind made her jump, and she raised her hands in front of her body again.

A large animal was tied to a post at the corner of her house. A horse, she told herself, reminded of the images she'd seen in one of her many books. With her mind on edge, the grand beast made her back away with fear.

Her pacing interrupted, she looked down at her prisoner to see his eyes blinking open. She readied her hands and watched as he fully opened them. He blinked a few more times and mumbled a few incoherent words before he noticed her. His eyes widened, and he tugged his hands forward, but the roots held firm.

"What?" he said with a grunt, still pulling at the roots that held him down.

Elice drew in a deep breath and forced her voice to sound deeper than normal. "Where's Lenore?"

The man stopped fussing with his bonds long enough to meet Elice's eyes. "Who?" he asked, a puzzled expression on his face.

"The person you stole that necklace from," she said, forcing out the words. "What did you do to her?"

"I didn't steal it from her," he mumbled, once again distracted by trying to break free. "I found it, and I came all the way out here to return it to her."

Elice narrowed her eyes. She wondered if he was telling the truth. Lifting her arms, the roots moved in time with her hands as they dug further into the man's arms and legs.

He groaned but otherwise hid his pain. For a moment, she wondered if she could keep this up—if she would be able to get answers from him.

She pursed her lips and held tight to the feeling of the roots as they dug into his skin. "Tell me where she is," she demanded.

"I don't know." He clenched his jaw.

She closed her fingers to make a fist, and the shoots around his limbs grew tighter. "Tell me the truth!"

"I am! I swear." He didn't bother hiding his agony anymore as a few drops of blood fell from the cuts on his wrists. "I just want to return the necklace to Madam Lenore and then I'll leave. I promise."

Elice paused, her mind going over what he said. He had called Lenore 'madam,' a term meant for the kingdom's most admired and revered mages. It had been out of use since the Last Mage War, so why did he use it to refer to the old woman?

She loosened the roots, and his face softened as the pain let up.

Shame crept its way through her mind as she realized how severe her reaction had been. It snaked around inside her chest, gripping her heart as tightly as the roots around the soldier's arms and legs. Her first interaction with another human being and she used it to prove Lenore right—she couldn't control her powers.

Spots of blood gathered around his wrists and ankles, so she willed herself to calm down. She did not want to be the person Lenore warned her she could become—an uncontrollable mage with wild powers. With her emotions in check, she kneeled beside the stranger and started pulling the roots away.

Once she freed one hand, he reached over and began ripping at the bindings around his other wrist. She sat back on her heels as he tore at the roots around his ankles. He returned her gaze with the same perplexed expression he had before.

Elice stood as he finished unraveling himself. When he finally stood, his legs wobbled underneath his body and he gripped his head in his hands. A thick vine cinched around her heart as she stared at him in his discomfort.

"She's not here," Elice said once she found her voice again.

The man sighed and shook his head, grimacing as he moved. "I'm having the worst day," he muttered. He rubbed the back of his head where she imagined a lump now formed. "It had started out so great."

She bit her lip before blurting out a genuine apology. "I'm sorry. I didn't mean to hurt you. I saw Lenore's necklace around your neck and thought something bad happened to her."

She drew in a deep breath, realizing how fast she had spoken. The man lifted an eyebrow as he chuckled at her outburst.

"I'm Andre," he said, placing his right palm over his heart.

She mimicked his gesture. "Elice."

Andre made a face, one Elice realized was of amusement or curiosity rather than confusion. "Elice," he repeated her name, as if trying the word out for the first time.

She nodded her head once. "You said my name earlier, which is what startled me."

"No, I said Alice." He shook his head and winced again.

"Well, it's pronounced Elice." She emphasized the first E in her name.

The young man stared for a moment before speaking again. "And your mother? What's her name?"

Elice shifted her feet, uncomfortable with this strange man's question. Lenore told her how her parents died, and it still hurt knowing she would never meet them. "My parents died in the war."

"Right," he said, this time nodding his head in agreement. "But you look just like her..." His eyes became distant, as if lost in some memory or thought too complex to recall with his wounded head.

"I think you should sit down for a bit. You must have hit your head pretty hard."

Andre's gaze snapped to hers. His breath caught in his throat, and his words faltered. "By the Fates! You... You're a mage! The roots and the wind—you hit me with wind!"

She lowered her face, knowing she could get in trouble for using magic. "I can't control my powers."

Andre took a step back. He looked at their surroundings, first taking in her disheveled clothes, then to the tiny cottage behind her, and finally the open field that surrounded her house. "Is that why you live here? Because you have magic?"

She thought he would turn and run away, fearful of what she revealed. Instead, he chuckled. "Well, at least I didn't die, and you stopped your torturous branches from snapping my limbs from my body. You must not be that dangerous."

Elice pointed at the bloodstains that still lingered on his skin, the sleeves of his green uniform doing nothing to hide them. "But I hurt you, and I think you might have a concussion."

An amused smile played on his lips. "I've had concussions before. Besides, you probably thought I was going to hurt you. If it had been me, I'm not sure I would have been able to control myself."

"Really?" Elice wondered if he was telling the truth. She only had Lenore as a reference for interpreting social cues, and the old woman wasn't very sociable.

He nodded. "Honestly."

"I need to find Lenore," she said. "She's weak without her talisman. I'm worried something might have happened to her."

"I found it in Highmore," Andre said, pulling the necklace over his head. "I accidentally bumped into her, and she dropped everything she was carrying, so I helped her pick up her things. That's when I saw this ... charm, as you called it, lying on the ground. When I looked up to hand it back to her, she was gone. I've been searching for her all day."

Elice reached forward and grabbed the chain. He opened his fist to release it from his grip. "How do you know my guardian?" she asked as she pulled the loop over her own head and let the charm settle on top of her chest.

"I've seen her around town a few times. Mainly avoided her since she's, well..." He looked between the charm and Elice's eyes. She found herself quite pleased when a carefree smile returned to his face.

"Scary. Yes, I know." She placed a finger on the charm as if caressing a long-lost toy, and it seemed to shimmer in appreciation. "Can you tell me how to get to Highmore?"

She had read about the tiny village surrounding the castle of Norraine. If Highmore was the last place Lenore had been, she at least had a starting point to begin her search. Elice would go against Lenore's warnings about not being in control of her magic if it meant she knew the old mage was safe.

Andre shook his head. "Highmore is a long way from here. It took me a couple hours to find this cottage, and I was riding a horse. It would take much longer if you were to walk."

Elice frowned. She hadn't thought about having to make a long journey. What if it took days to find Lenore? Her seventeenth birthday was now only nine days away.

"But I can take you to Highmore," Andre began, "so long as you promise not to knock me off my horse with a typhoon."

She couldn't make any promises, not when she spent her entire life being told she was a threat to those around her. Elice couldn't predict her magic, especially if her emotions ran high. "I can't—I shouldn't. I don't know you, and you don't know what I'm capable of."

He laughed. "We should change that, then. I'm Andre, Lord of Copita, faithful servant of King Edgar the Defender, and a

Lieutenant in the King's Army." He gave an exaggerated bow that Elice knew was too fancy for someone like her.

"I'm..." She hesitated, not knowing how to respond to his spectacle. "Just Elice."

Andre chuckled again. "Well, *Elice*, Master of the Elements, I believe we have gotten to know each other very well over the last several minutes."

Elice shook her head, but she couldn't stop the smile that found its way to her lips.

"Besides," he continued, "when was the last time you left this forest?"

"I've never actually left." She looked down at her feet again. She was still barefoot, which made her feel self-conscious for the first time in her life.

"Wait, is Madam Lenore keeping you prisoner here?"

"No, it's not like that."

"Then what's the problem?" His question was lighthearted, as if he couldn't see a problem.

"First," Elice began, knowing this man had no clue how powerful she was. "I can't control my magic."

He hummed and furrowed his eyebrows in thought. "That could be a problem. You really could knock me off my horse."

"Second, Lenore would never forgive me if I left the cottage, especially if I put someone else in danger."

"Minor issue." Andre waved his hand.

"And last, as I'm sure you know, magic is forbidden."

He quirked an eyebrow before laughing again. "If those are your only concerns, I suggest we hurry and leave before we lose precious daylight." He walked to his horse and gave it a few pats along its side.

She had never been so confused before in her life. This man seemed so carefree, which was the exact opposite of how Elice felt inside. She could feel the nerves rush through her like a shock of electricity as she contemplated leaving. This would be the riskiest thing she had ever done. She compared it to the time she told Lenore she hated her porridge—which resulted in Elice being the sole cook in the house. That moment paled in comparison, and she knew Lenore would be even more upset with her this time.

But what other choice did she have? Lenore could be suffering, growing weaker every minute without her talisman's protection, and Elice stood there worrying her time away instead of taking action.

She nodded to herself before she rushed into her small house and grabbed her shoes—the only pair she had, full of mud stains and holes.

When she stepped outside, Andre had already unhitched his horse and placed a brimmed cap on his head. He looked at her with a wide grin, one she couldn't help but return. "So, you've decided to come."

"On one condition." Elice hesitated to walk any closer to the massive horse. "You help me find Lenore."

The amusement fell from his expression. His eyes darkened, and he was once again lost in his thoughts. Elice could almost see a dozen images flash before his eyes.

He nodded and placed his hand over his heart. "By my honor and by the Fates' design, I will help you find who you're looking for."

Elice smiled. *This is it*, she thought, as she cautiously approached the horse to ride away from her home for the first time.

"Don't worry. Oro's a gentle giant. I'll hop on first to show you how it's done."

She nodded as he showed her where to place her foot in the stirrup. With a leap, he pulled himself onto the horse's saddle. After he settled, he extended his hand for her to grab.

Elice took in a breath before she placed her hand in his. She slid a foot into the stirrup, then kicked off the ground with her other foot as he hauled her up. Holding on to the back of his shirt, she balanced herself on the horse's back.

"See," he said over his shoulder, "that wasn't so bad." He grabbed the reins and gave the horse a kick with his heels.

As the horse set off at a slow trot, Elice gripped the back of the saddle and looked behind her. She often wished her life would change, and now it was happening so fast she didn't have time to think about it.

Soon, the open field led to the edge of the Jani Forest. Tall trees reached high above their heads and blocked out the sun's natural light. They passed by several thick rows of trees until Elice couldn't see her lonely cottage anymore. She faced forward, pursed her lips, and focused on the sound of the horse's clatter.

Three

"So, what's it like?" Andre asked after several minutes.

"What's what like?" Elice tried to look at him, but she couldn't see much of his face from her position.

"Being a mage. I've never met one before. I don't count Madam Lenore since I've never really talked to her. There must be many others out there, but they can't reveal what they are otherwise people will accuse them of using magic."

Elice sat in silence for a moment. What did it feel like to be a mage? She never gave it much thought other than trying to control her powers. "I'm not exactly what you would call a normal mage."

She felt Andre shift in front of her. "Do tell."

"Well, Lenore's always told me I was born with special powers. I can control more than one element."

"And that's not normal?"

Elice adjusted in her seat. Her legs weren't used to being in such an uncomfortable position for so long. "Not at all. Most mages only use one power. Lenore brought me a book about the famous mages in history who could control two, though even that's rare. I can control three: air, earth, and water."

"So, you're a super mage?"

Elice laughed at the humor in his voice. "I wouldn't say that, since I'm supposed to be learning how to control my powers and *not* use them. But I can't. I feel so much better when I use them—when I let my powers run free."

"But Madam Lenore said you can't?" The question in his voice hung in the air, with a sharp edge to it that made Elice become defensive.

"It's against the law. And I've hurt her before. When I was younger, I didn't follow her directions to clear my mind before practicing. I got angry and struck at her with water magic. I almost flooded the entire cottage."

"That actually sounds kind of fun."

This time, Elice rolled her eyes as Andre laughed.

They traveled for over an hour by the time the trees thinned, and Elice could make out a path worn out by years of travel. The dirt path cut through the forest as if many travelers before them had walked this path over the centuries. Sprawling green trees full of life spread their branches out over the path, providing shelter from the summer sun.

Andre turned his head so Elice could see part of his face. "I think I have the beginning of a plan. I'll take you to a shop I know in town. The woman who owns it sells medicine—herbs and such—and she knows Madam Lenore. In fact, she's the one who told me where I might find Madam Lenore's cottage. I think she'll have more information, if we can get to her before she closes for the night."

Elice nodded in agreement, the excitement growing in her stomach. "I can't wait to see Highmore. I've read books about the kingdom—well, I read anything Lenore brought me so I could pass the time. Is the city big?"

"It's mainly just shops and small houses for the locals. The main appeal is the castle in the backdrop. I'm still in awe every time I see it."

She could feel the gleam in her eyes as she envisioned riding up to the tall gates surrounding the city, with Highmore castle lit up in the background. "You said you're the lord of Copita? That's not far from Highmore, right?"

"Not far at all. It's the closest city to the capital. I guess I'm lucky that way."

"You must be close to the king if he made you a lord."

He rubbed the back of his hat, pulling it down before readjusting it. "My father died in the Last Mage War. As his only child, I was left in charge of the estate. Of course, I was only a baby at the time, so my mother managed it until this year when I turned seventeen." He paused as if he wanted to say more, but he cleared his throat and continued in silence.

After another hour, they made it out of the forest and into a large field. Elice couldn't see much ahead of them except for green grass that grew several inches off the ground. On the horizon to the west, the sun was getting low, and she knew the shops would close soon.

It only took a few more minutes before a stone wall appeared in the distance. As they grew closer, she realized they were approaching the walled-in city of Highmore.

An immense fortress protected the city. The walls were larger than Elice ever imagined. The iron gates stood open even at such a late hour. Metal gates connected on either side to massive stone towers. The guards on duty were only just visible from Elice's position on the ground below.

Andre pulled the horse to a stop just outside the main entry and carefully slid off, then helped Elice do the same. She held his hands and allowed him to guide her off the horse. The way down was less graceful than she intended, with her legs and bottom sore from the two-hour horseback ride. Her legs were useless, and she fell into Andre's waiting arms. He caught her, steadying her movements as her legs failed to comply with her commands.

"I got you," he said with a smile, one that Elice stared at for too long. "It was a long ride, especially for someone who has never ridden a horse before."

Elice smiled as he helped her stand upright. "Thanks for catching me."

Andre grinned as he turned toward the capital city and raised his arms. "Here we are! Your first trip to the citadel. The guards will shut the gates soon, though, so we should hurry. The shop we're looking for is just inside the main gates."

He pulled the horse by the reins a few steps before halting. Elice, still walking on wobbly limbs, crashed into him. "I almost forgot." He turned, pulling his green military coat from his shoulders and removing his hat, then passed both to Elice. "You might want to put these on."

"Why?" asked Elice, eyeing the articles of clothing as she grabbed them.

"I don't know how to explain it, but you look exactly like someone—someone from Highmore."

She slid the jacket on and donned the large hat. It covered her eyes as it slid over the front of her head. "Who do I look like?"

One side of his mouth turned up in a nervous grin. "The princess."

"The princess? Of Norraine?" Her eyebrows shot into her forehead beneath the hat.

Andre pulled on his ear. "I've been trying to find a way to tell you. The resemblance is uncanny. I wouldn't want someone to confuse you with her. That would raise too many questions that we don't have the answers to."

"What questions?"

"Well, for one, why do you look like a member of the royal family?" He adjusted the cap on her head, pulling it further down to hide more of her face. "This will have to do for now."

He shrugged, then motioned with his hand for her to walk ahead. They continued side-by-side, and Andre placed one hand on her elbow to guide her through the gates and the other he used to pull Oro's reins.

Elice's attention soon diverted to the matching towers on either side of her. With the brim of his hat blocking her view, she had to tilt her head toward the darkening sky to take in as much of the towering structures as she could. She stared in awe at their size. The gray stones created two circular columns, with a guard post resting on top nearly three stories high.

They continued past the towers, where rows of shops and trade stores lined the right and left side of a large, cobbled path. Directly on her left was a bakery, and Elice caught a whiff of the glorious pastries and breads that sat on display in the front window. She inhaled the sweet scent, wishing this was the shop they were looking for.

Elice caught Andre staring at her, and she became self-conscious in his presence again. Of course the town would seem mundane to someone like him since he must have passed by these shops dozens of times. This made her aware of just how secluded her life had been before this moment. She cleared her throat to hide her embarrassment and turned from his amused stare.

The streets were quieter than Elice imagined them to be, with only a few citizens communing outside of stores or wandering the walkway. She pictured what the citadel would be like during daylight hours, with the normal hustle and bustle of the crowd and merchants selling their wares at the now-empty wagons that occupied spots along the path.

They came to a stop in front of a small shop. Elice looked around the exterior of the storefront to find a sign. When she found nothing, she turned to Andre. "Is this it?"

He answered with a nod as he tied Oro's reins to a post outside the building. "It's good that we arrived so late. We should be able to get in, gather the information, and leave without causing a scene. Now, when we walk in, stay toward the back of the shop. Try not to let anyone see your face."

Together, they entered the store and the bell above the door chimed. Elice could feel the magical energy as soon as she walked in, the source no doubt coming from the various knickknacks throughout the space. She wondered if the shop owner was a mage and sold these items knowing the non-mages wouldn't be able to feel their magical properties.

Andre pointed to a shelf near the entrance, and she acknowledged him by walking toward it. She rummaged through the various vials and other items that lined the shelf as Andre walked to the front counter.

Out of the corner of her eye, she noticed a door slide open from the left side of the room. She looked up just as Andre approached the counter.

"I see you made it back safely," said the woman who came up to greet him. She had a kind, soothing voice and long, coiled curls with a few gray strands peeking through. The woman's eyes roamed the store before meeting Elice's. Elice lowered her gaze and picked up the first thing she saw on the shelf. She pretended to show interest in the small pouch labeled *birch bark* before relegating it to an empty slot. She picked up another pouch, though she continued to listen to the conversation across the room.

"Yeah, about that," she heard Andre say. "I came across, well, a hitch."

"You didn't find the house?"

"I found the house, but Madam Lenore wasn't there."

"That's good news. I warned you to stay away from that old woman. You can't trust her. You should let the matter go while you still have the chance."

Elice's eyebrows furrowed together at the shop owner's words.

She looked at the woman again and noticed the intense stare she gave Andre. Why was this woman trying so hard to convince him to stay away from Lenore?

Andre turned his head to glance at Elice. The shop owner followed his gaze, and Elice looked down again before they could make eye contact. She forced herself to turn toward the shelf behind her and grabbed another pouch, this one labeled *blue sage*.

"It's too late for that, Madam Olivia," said Andre, returning to his conversation. "Which is why I'm here. I came to ask if you have any other information on Madam Lenore."

"I told you all I know," the woman answered.

"But you must know more. Another contact, perhaps? Is there anyone else who might know where she is?"

"As I told you before, no one crosses paths with that woman. Nothing good comes from being associated with her, so stop your search now before something bad happens."

Elice jammed the pouch of sage sticks back on the ledge. Why was this woman saying such horrible things about her guardian? Was this person even talking about the same Lenore? Sure, Lenore was harsh, and she showed no affection toward Elice, but Lenore was the closest thing she had to family. Elice didn't like hearing someone talk badly about Lenore.

"I hear your warnings, Madam Olivia." She heard Andre sigh.

"I'm not sure you understand what I'm trying to say, young man. If you knew half the things she's done—well, all I can say is she's just evil."

Unable to hold her tongue any longer, Elice stormed to the counter, ignoring the shocked looks on the faces before her as she removed the hat from her head and slammed it on the counter.

"How dare you?" she yelled. "You know nothing about her! What makes you say such horrible things?" Andre and the woman stared with mouths agape as the wind began whipping around them, blowing loose sheets of paper across the counter and around the room. Elice knew she shouldn't erupt, though she couldn't help but defend the woman who raised her.

Andre groaned beside her. Still, she held the woman's gaze, only blinking when her curls blew aver her eyes. Madam Olivia's eyes peered into her own, and her senses pulled as the older woman tried to read through Elice's expression. Elice understood that this woman had magic—she must be a healer because, little by little, she could feel her anger and anxiety dissipate as they maintained eye contact. Slowly, her anger calmed to a slow boil until she relaxed enough to stop the air from flying around.

Before this moment, she had only ever read about the power of a healer. Experiencing it now for the first time, she knew why, before the war, healers were the most respected mages. They could reduce pain and treat wounds with the touch of a hand. They understood how to mix different ingredients to create healing ointments and potions. And, as Elice realized, they could take away a person's fear and anger with only a focused stare. Elice wished she would have been born a healer instead of the abomination she was.

The healer nodded her head as if, in that moment of fixed gaze with Elice, she understood everything Elice felt. Madam Olivia closed her eyes for a moment before she sighed, the sound coming out as strong as a gust of wind.

"I cannot help you," the woman began, opening her eyes once

more to look at Elice. "Madam Lenore only stays in town for a day, and then she's off again. I don't know where she goes after leaving my shop as I never ask questions—I doubt anyone else knows much about her, either."

Andre, who had his head buried in the palms of his hands, stood straight and shook his head. "Thank you for your time, Madam Olivia." He grabbed his hat from the counter and motioned for Elice to follow him out of the store.

Elice took a step backward, then stopped, caught with one foot behind her and one ahead of her. She wanted to ask the woman more questions since she had never met another mage besides Lenore. She heard the door to the shop open, and she turned her head to see Andre waiting for her to leave with him. Resigned, she turned to leave as well. Now wasn't the time for curiosity. She needed to remain focused on finding Lenore.

"Be careful," she heard Madam Olivia call out as she reached the door. She looked over her shoulder at the healer. "Be careful who you trust, young one."

Andre placed his hand on Elice's elbow and guided her out of the shop before she could respond.

"Well, that was a wasted effort," Andre said as they walked out into the night. Darkness settled around them now as the sun fell beneath the horizon. Lanterns lit the street from tall posts, just bright enough to see a few feet in front of them as they walked.

Store owners busied themselves with closing up their shops, calling out to each other as they wished their neighbors a peaceful night. Still, a few patrons gathered in small groups beside lanterns, laughing and winding down from their day.

Elice stared at the stones beneath her battered shoes. She wondered what she would do next—she was nowhere closer to finding Lenore than before leaving her cottage. What if Lenore was already home, and Elice had overreacted when she saw her guardian's talisman?

I never should have left, she thought. I should have stayed home instead of coming all this way for nothing.

She opened her mouth to apologize to Andre for having wasted his time, but he spoke first.

"Listen," he began, heading to his horse to untie its reins. "It's too late to do anything else now. We should head to my estate and pick up our search in the morning."

"Wait." She paused, coming to a stop beside the horse. "You still want to help me?"

"Well, I brought you all this way. Besides, I don't plan on letting you wander the forest—alone, at night."

"Here I was, blaming myself," she muttered. "But what if we have worse luck tomorrow?"

"I have an idea about that." He motioned toward the city's gates. "First thing tomorrow, I promise, we'll continue our search. I think I'll take you to the castle so you can meet the princess you resemble so much."

Elice followed him out of the gates. "How will meeting the princess help me in my search?"

Once outside the gate, Andre jumped on Oro's back and reached his hand forward to help Elice. He hauled her up and let her get comfortable before he spoke again. "I have this weird feeling you'll find all your answers and more in the castle."

"No offense, Andre, but you aren't making much sense. I think I made you hit your head way too hard."

Andre looked over his shoulder and gave her a lopsided smile before nudging his horse with his heel.

Four

I t was a short hour ride to Andre's estate in Copita. The dirt
path to the village was well worn and lit by several metal
lantern posts every few feet. All around her, the animals of the
night made their presence known, from the small crickets chirping
to the large owls hooting. A gentle breeze blew, calming her mind
as she thought about the day's events.

Andre slowed his horse to a quiet trot as they turned off the main
path and onto a stone walkway large enough for four horses to
walk across side-by-side. "I think we should come up with a cover
story for when we bring you to the castle."

In the distance, Elice could see the Copita estate. It shone in the
darkness by several lamps placed along the outside walls. "I can't
be just Elice?"

He shook his head. "Unfortunately, no. There will be so many
people there, and if anyone gets a good look at your face, rumors

are bound to spread. We could say you're the princess's distant cousin? No, the servants might alert the whole castle that a relative is visiting. We'll just say you're my cousin, very distant, and just shrug off your resemblance to anyone who brings it up."

"Will that work?" They stopped in front of a gray brick staircase leading up to the front door. Elice could see the dark wood of the door, a deep brown that reminded her of the black tea she would make with the leftover leaves Lenore brought home from her trips. A silver doorknob adorned the middle of it, and a stained-glass window took up the top portion. It swung open, silencing whatever reply Andre had.

Elice saw an old man exit as Andre slipped out of the saddle, raising his hands to take her waist. Having learned from her previous attempt at dismounting, Elice leaned into his hands, which allowed him to set her on the ground without slipping.

Rushing down the stairs with surprising agility, the older man with pale gray hair greeted them. Despite his age, the man stood proud and tall as he adjusted the collar of his crisp white shirt underneath his half-buttoned black coat. His matching trousers appeared pressed and had a crease running from each hip to the cuff of his shiny black boots. She expected to hear a raspy voice, but the man spoke with an almost regal demeanor. "My Lord, you were not expected back this evening. Shall I have the cook prepare your dinner?"

"Yes, please do, Mr. Wade," Andre responded. Someone else rushed out of the house and ran straight to Oro. He wore a baggy tan shirt and tattered cloth pants, which he rubbed his hands across as if trying to wipe off dirt. Andre passed the reins to the boy, who appeared to be a couple of years younger than Elice. "Please see that Oro gets plenty of food and water. He's had a long journey."

"Right away, sir," the boy said, tugging on the reins and guiding the horse to the side of the house. Elice watched as they disappeared behind a tall topiary along the corner of the house. She assumed they were headed to the stables, and she hoped to get a glimpse of it before they left in the morning.

Elice's attention returned to Andre when he said her name. He motioned toward her as he spoke to Mr. Wade. "This is my cousin, from a small fishing village in Corvet. A room will need to be prepared for her to freshen up since we've been traveling all day. We'll visit the castle after breakfast tomorrow, so she'll need proper attire as well."

She didn't know if this story would work since she wore such a shabby dress and was definitely worse-for-wear after being on the back of a horse for the better part of the evening.

To her surprise and relief, the man gave a low bow. "Very good, my lord. I shall have a maid prepare a room immediately and see to having her properly dressed." After another quick nod and bow, Mr. Wade stepped aside to allow Elice and Andre to enter the house. Andre gestured with his arm for Elice to step inside first.

As soon as she entered, Elice took in the scene before her. The entrance hall had dozens of candles resting inside ornate silver sconces, which hung on the walls and illuminated the entry. They also lined the hallways, allowing her to see how high the ceilings were. Paintings of people dressed in elegant outfits adorned the cream-colored walls. Ceramic vases with giant topiaries that matched the one outside sat in every corner she could see.

She followed Andre a few steps further to where two luxurious ivory couches sat across from each other. Elice ran a hand along the surface, noting how soft the material felt beneath her skin. Matching pillows lay in a pattern across the cushions. Looking down, she took in the highly polished stone floor that reflected the light from the lanterns.

Another person appeared at her side, this time a girl around her own age. "May I take your coat, ma'am?" the girl asked. Elice noticed she had a strange accent, different from Mr. Wade's, and even Andre's. It took Elice a moment to understand what she said. The girl stared at her a moment longer before Elice snapped to attention, removing Andre's coat and passing it to her.

Andre cleared his throat. "Dahlia, please show our guest to her room."

"Right away, my lord," answered Dahlia. She turned to Elice and motioned toward a staircase on the left. They walked up the stairs and through a long hallway. More paintings hung on the walls, with different people and sometimes even beautiful nature scenes. Sconces lit the way, which helped her watch her footsteps on the plush cream carpet.

They soon reached a white door. Dahlia opened it, then stood aside for Elice to enter first.

Dahlia walked in after her and started lighting a few candles. Once it was bright enough, Elice looked around the room. In the middle sat a grand bed with four tall posts, one on each corner. This bed was so large it wouldn't even fit in the small living room of her cottage. A lush carpet lay on the floor at the foot of the bed.

A vanity with a padded stool sat to her right. In the back of the room, a wooden wardrobe and another door took up the entire wall.

"I'll draw your bath first, my lady," said the maid, bringing Elice out of her wonderment. "Then I'll find you some fresh clothes. Should be something about your size."

She smiled at Elice before heading to the door in the back. Elice followed her and walked into a bathroom. The same glossy stone used downstairs lined the bathroom floors and walls, causing the room to shine with the reflection of the candlelight.

Standing in the middle of this glorious room, her mouth dropped open in awe. A massive tub took up most of the space, with a table to her right holding a porcelain bowl and a toilet in the far-left corner.

A chuckle escaped her mouth as Dahlia turned on the spigot and filled the tub with warm water. At home, she had to gather the water herself, either from the well by the outhouse or with magic to heat it up in a pot over a fire. As soon as Dahlia left, Elice threw off her clothes, wanting to jump into the tub as soon as possible.

Sighing, she sank into the warmth of the mesmerizing water. She reached for a bar of soap that rested on the ledge of the tub and started lathering. A few minutes in the tub would be all right, she reasoned with herself. She would take some time to indulge in this extravagant pleasure before returning downstairs.

When she finished, she used a thick towel to dry off, relishing in its comfort before she wrapped it around her body and left the bathroom. Dahlia had already hung several dresses in the wardrobe and was busying herself with arranging shoes on the bottom shelf of the closet.

"I've brought you a few dresses to choose from, ma'am," she said, standing from her knelt position.

"Thanks, Dahlia," Elice responded, walking toward the articles of clothing. Many of the choices were long, billowy yellow garments that looked too difficult to get into by herself. She pulled one dress at a time from their spot on the rack, feeling the softness of the cloth and wishing to feel them against her skin.

A pale-yellow dress caught her eye, and she removed it from its hanger. She held it against her body and looked down, smiling as she envisioned wearing it. "I like this one," she said, looking back at Dahlia.

With the maid's help, Elice squeezed into the dress. She stood before the vanity and barely recognized herself. Besides the curly mass of hair that went all the way down her back, she looked—and felt—like a different person.

The dress fit her perfectly. It hugged her in curves she never noticed she had underneath the old cloth she used to think was a dress. She now realized it was a sack in comparison. Dahlia grabbed a pair of white sandals that strapped around the ankles, and Elice slipped them on, appreciating the way they felt on her feet. Then she went back to the bathroom for Lenore's charm necklace and pulled it over her neck, resting it against her chest. At least she had one thing from home.

Taking a deep breath, she followed the maid out of the room. They returned to the main living space, and Dahlia motioned to the white couches before excusing herself.

Elice made her way toward the couches in the middle of the

room but hesitated to sit on them in case they were only for show—it looked as if no one ever sat on them. She resigned to walk around the edge of the room where a bookcase rested against the wall. It was larger and had dozens more books than her own shelves at the cottage. She reached out, wanting to grab a book to immerse herself in while she waited for Andre, but a painting in the middle of the wall grabbed her attention.

A gasp slipped from her open mouth. Elice took a step closer. She couldn't believe what she saw—she couldn't believe *who* she saw. The painting was a portrait of a woman wearing a yellow dress with a yellow and white bow tied around her waist. At first, Elice thought she saw herself painted in that portrait, but as she took another step closer, she noticed subtle differences between herself and the painting's subject.

The other person's hair was shorter, just below her shoulders—Elice's hair hadn't been that short since she was ten years old. The curls were different as well—they had less bounce and were thicker. The skin tone was also a bit lighter than Elice's rich brown tone. Most notably, the subject's smile was tiny, a slight upward curve of the lips that seemed rather uncomfortable instead of happy. This person seemed awkward, as if she was shy and didn't wish to share a smile.

At the bottom corner was the artist's signature—a large letter A and a scribble at the end marking a last name Elice couldn't decipher. Beneath the signature was a note:

Self-portrait of Alice of House Moore, Crown Princess of Norraine

Year 324.

~for Andre Lee of Copita.

Heart pounding, Elice read the year again, realizing the artist had painted it within the past year. She wondered why the princess would paint a self-portrait and gift it to Andre. She thought it even more strange that Andre would hang this large painting in the middle of his living room for all to see. The strangest thing of all was how the princess looked almost exactly like her.

A door on the opposite side of the room opened and Elice whipped around, her nerves on edge. Andre entered the room with an enormous smile, but it faltered when he saw Elice. His gaze passed between her and the portrait behind her, his eyes darting back and forth.

"Ah, yes," he muttered, stepping completely into the room. "I see you found the portrait."

"That's not me," she blurted, but the statement sounded more like a question. She wanted to make sure it wasn't her face on the wall behind her.

"No, it's not you," he answered. He took another hesitant step forward.

"It's the princess?" Another question, just to confirm what she knew.

"Crown Princess Alice, daughter of King Edgar and Queen

Julice." He spoke slowly, as if Elice would miss the words as they left his lips. She missed nothing, though—not the names of royal family members, or how they sounded in her head, echoing inside her brain.

"Alice," she repeated aloud. "Julice."

"And Elice," he finished for her.

"What..." She wanted to ask another question, but she didn't know what to say.

"What, indeed." Andre took several more steps until he stood a few feet away from her. "I don't know what's going on, and you're right: I think I hit my head pretty hard. But I'm beginning to think there's more going on here than we originally thought. Again, it could be the concussion."

"And you think I should just abandon my search for Lenore to go to the castle? Is that what you've been planning?" She narrowed her eyes, seeing behind his lie.

"We have no leads on Madam Lenore's whereabouts. It seems no one will give us any information about her, if they even have any idea themselves. And I have a feeling we're supposed to go to the castle."

She placed her hands on her hips. "You have a feeling? Do you have magic now?"

He chuckled and crossed his arms over his chest. "When's your birthday?"

Elice didn't know why he asked such a question. When she remained quiet, he continued. "The princess's seventeenth birthday is in nine days. When's your birthday, Elice?"

She dropped her arms, letting them hang limply at her sides. Her apprehension must have shown on her face, because he nodded his head and walked to stand in front of her. "It's in nine days, as well. Just as I thought."

"What are you saying?" She didn't want him to say it. She didn't want to hear it. She wanted to cover her ears and run from the room, out of the mansion, and all the way through the woods until she was safe inside her dark, tiny cottage in the middle of nowhere.

Yet she remained rooted to her spot. She had to hear what he thought, to see if he was thinking the same thing she was.

"I don't think your parents are dead."

Five

So many thoughts ran amok in Elice's head. If her parents weren't dead, then Lenore lied to her. Why would she do such a thing? Lenore was grim and as hard as a rock, but Elice never thought of her as a liar. Sure, the woman kept secrets and didn't explain everything she did or what she saw in her visions. That didn't mean she was as untrustworthy as the shop owner said, did it?

She thought of the time she found a frog in her garden and brought it inside the cottage to keep as a pet, only to have Lenore snatch the animal from her hands to throw it outside—Lenore told her she could never have a pet. She remembered her eighth birthday, one of the many she'd spent alone because Lenore wouldn't bring her along on her travels, and how she ate stale bread instead of a birthday cake. She thought of the aching loneliness that etched scars on her heart with every passing day, wondering if she would ever leave that desolate cottage.

Elice refused to think what it meant if Lenore hadn't told her the truth about her parents.

Mr. Wade entered the room, bringing Elice back to the present. "Dinner is ready, my lord."

"Thank you, Mr. Wade," Andre said. He caught Elice's eye, but she turned and walked into the room behind Mr. Wade, coming into a dining room with an eight-seat table. Atop the table, a pair of candelabras held three candles each, and crisp white tableware and silver utensils were placed at both ends. The servants only set enough for two people to eat.

A servant offered to pull out her chair, but Elice pulled it before he could get the chance to. She sat with a plop, her mind still reeling and her heart beating faster than she'd ever felt.

The servant set a slightly smaller plate on top of the original, this one filled with food. This reminded her of the empty feeling in her stomach. She grabbed a fork and brought it to her plate. Her eyes widened at the plump, juicy tomatoes and fresh, big-leafed greens. The small garden she maintained at the cottage didn't produce fruits and vegetables as beautiful or appetizing as what was currently before her.

She looked up at the sound of Andre's laugh. "We have amazing farmers here in Copita. The best in the land. We even supply food for the residents of Highmore."

At the mention of Highmore, both her appetite and stomach shrunk in size.

Andre cleared his throat and waited for the servants to leave the dining room before speaking again. "Listen, I know this may be a bit overwhelming—"

"Overwhelming," Elice interjected, stabbing a tomato in the process. "First, you show up at my doorstep wearing my guardian's necklace, claiming to have found it. Then you bring me to a foreign city where I don't know anyone, in a poor attempt at finding said guardian, who I'm worried about because she is old and sickly. And now you try to tell me there's some strange connection between me and the princess of Norraine." She bit the piece of red fruit and placed her fork on the table.

Andre wiped his mouth with the corner of a white napkin, but Elice caught the tiny smile he was trying to hide. "That about sums it up, yes."

"I don't understand how you can smile at a time like this." She sat back in her chair and stared at the man before her with a confused expression.

"I'm just curious, is all. I'd like to find out what's going on as much as you."

She picked her fork up again, eating a small bite of lettuce. Her eyes continued to meet Andre's from across the table. "Why would the Princess give you a self-portrait?"

He took his time chewing, then gave a hard swallow. "Oh. We're engaged." He continued eating as if he hadn't spoken at all.

Elice didn't expect his answer, but she had only known this man for less than a day, which meant she didn't know him at all. What did it matter to her if he was engaged to the princess—other than their matching faces? She tried not to think about how weird it was that Andre didn't seem to want to talk about it.

She raised an eyebrow and continued to press him. "Why didn't you mention earlier that you were engaged to the princess?"

"I'm not sure." He shrugged, still staring at his plate of food. "Maybe because we've been best friends since we were children and have been engaged for only a year. I still think of her as a friend more than anything else."

He met her eyes, and Elice could see the conflict swirling around in them. She wanted to know what he was thinking, but the expression disappeared as quickly as it had appeared. Elice remained quiet, watching Andre from across the table with a careful eye.

After dinner, Dahlia showed her to her room again. She had laid out some nightclothes and folded down the sheets. After helping her out of the gown, Dahlia bid her goodnight and left her alone.

In her nightgown, Elice slid under the soft white sheets and almost sunk into the lush blankets.

Her mind refused to slow down as she lay in the massive bed, tossing and turning to find a comfortable position. In truth, the bed was too comfortable and reminded her of how she wasn't sleeping in her old cot tonight.

As dawn neared, she still found herself unable to sleep. She contemplated leaving many times throughout the night, but she had so many questions that needed answers. Andre was right—she was likely to find those answers inside Highmore Castle, with the girl who's face looked like hers. Yet the implications that came with finding out why they looked so much alike kept her stomach in knots.

When the sun made its ascent into the sky, Elice rolled out of the luxurious bed she found no comfort in and got dressed. She wore a long dark-blue dress today, unable to get rid of the image of the princess's yellow dress from the self-portrait. Tucked into the collar of her dress was Lenore's necklace, the cold metal chain resting against her skin.

Andre was already awake—she saw him lounging on a couch in the main room, reading from a sheet of paper. He heard her approaching and set the paper beside him on the cushion.

He smiled and stood as she entered the room. "You look beautiful," he said. He reached for one of her hands and gently clasped it in both of his.

She smiled at the compliment. It was the first time someone called her beautiful, considering Lenore wasn't too fond of compliments. He guided her back to the dining room, to the same spot she had sat in last night. Fresh fruit, soft muffins, and clear glasses of water sat within grabbing distance from her chair.

With her stomach still twisted, she grabbed a muffin and picked a crumb from the top of it. She plopped it into her mouth, tasting the sweet banana flavor. While the delicious pastry would've enticed her on a different day, she couldn't bear to eat much of it.

"You seem nervous." Andre said, noticing her mood.

Elice dropped her muffin on the plate. "I'm about to meet the crown princess, and we have the same face. Of course I'm nervous. Besides, I can't stop thinking about Lenore. If she's made it back home, I know she'll be furious with me for leaving."

"There's nothing you can do now but continue down this path of truth." He shrugged and continued eating.

She nodded, although she was wary about the truth she sought in the first place.

After they finished breakfast, they headed for the door. Andre found Elice a dark blue cloak and told her to pull the hood far enough over her head to cover her face. She worried people might find her suspicious since it was early summer and there was no sensible reason for one to wear a hood. He waved this away, saying no one would question anyone who traveled with him.

This proved to be true as they rode Oro out of Copita and into the capital city. In the daylight, the citadel was even more stunning. She caught a few shop owners preparing for the day as they opened windows and doors and placed their various goods on shelves outside their store's windows. The carts that were empty last night now held a variety of merchandise, from jewelry and clothing to foods and drinks.

Patrons lined the street, doing some early morning shopping or catching up with their neighbors. As they passed a fountain in the center of the rectangular plaza, several children ran around the cobbled ground, playing a game of chase and laughing with each other.

She wanted to look over her shoulder to take in more of the town's sights, but the castle soon came into view. If she thought the estate of Copita was impressive, it paled in comparison to Highmore Castle's grand scale.

The gate they passed through was taller than the one outside of the main city. Andre slowed Oro to a stop so they could dismount before the gate. Elice held the edges of her hood with one hand so it wouldn't fall back as Andre helped her off the horse. The stone path from the town had ended, leading to a smooth, cement pavement wide enough for a large carriage to pass across.

They walked past a few guards in uniform, and they all nodded at Andre. One stepped forward, took Oro by the reins, and led the horse away. As they continued, she looked up to find the castle before her. Still holding on to her hood, she stared at the impeccable stonework. Individual square bricks were placed together like the pieces of a puzzle to create an intricate offset pattern running along the entire outer wall. She could see four columns that seemed to reach for the clouds, each facing one of the cardinal directions.

They walked toward the main entrance to a set of wooden double doors, the color a light brown tone, with curved gold handles. A young man in a military uniform appeared at their side and came to a halt. He raised a hand to his chest in the customary greeting.

Andre returned the gesture, placing his hand on his chest. "At ease, Thomas," was Andre's response. The man nodded and continued on his way.

Andre jogged his way up the stairs and opened the massive front doors for Elice. He stopped the first person he saw—Elice guessed it was a servant because of the tan uniform they wore. "Please send for Princess Alice. Tell her Lord Copita has brought a cousin to meet her. We'll be in the council room."

Elice didn't get the chance to look at the interior of the palace's main entry before Andre ushered her by the elbow along a hallway and through another extensive set of double doors.

"We'll wait in here," he said after he closed the doors. "This is a meeting room, though the council won't convene until the afternoon."

Elice felt herself nod. Her nerves threatened to make her stomach empty what little she ate for breakfast if she were to open her mouth. Instead of talking, she paced the room, ignoring its contents and Andre.

After several minutes, the doors swung open. She paused her pacing and stared at the person who entered. Her heart beat loudly in her chest as a girl wearing a yellow and cream dress walked into the room. Andre stood from where he was resting on one of the wing-backed chairs—Elice didn't even realize there were chairs in this room—and walked around the oval desk to meet her.

"There you are," the girl said, her voice soft. "I was so worried when you didn't show for dinner last night."

Elice lost her breath as she stared at the princess, their resemblance even more astonishing in person. Elice noticed they had the same nose and eyes—the girl's eyes narrowed with concern, just as Elice's did when she was worried. The only difference was the hair. She looked at the light brown waves throughout the princess's hair and how they hung delicately on her head.

Andre held the princess's hands. "I didn't mean to worry you. I couldn't explain at the time, but I had to do something really important. Remember when we went into town to get you more art supplies? Well, after I left you with the guards, I sort of ran into someone..."

"I'm just glad you're safe," the princess said, "and that you brought a family member for me to meet."

They both turned to Elice. She didn't know what to say—she still felt like she might throw up. Instead of speaking, she reached for the hood of the blue cloak and lowered it to her shoulders. She brushed her dark curls away from her face and they cascaded down to her hips as they fell out of the hood. She met the other girl's eyes, which widened as they stared at each other.

Andre stepped forward. "All right, don't freak out. Alice, meet Elice. Elice, this is Princess Alice."

Elice closed the distance. Even though her legs shook with each step, she wanted to see the other girl up close.

"Dre," the princess said, "what's going on?" Her voice trembled as she maintained eye contact with Elice.

"That's what we're here to find out," he answered.

The princess took a tentative step forward and whispered, "Who are you?"

"I..." Elice stuttered. She didn't know how to answer that question—she didn't really know who she was, and she couldn't tell the princess she was a mage, which was the only thing she knew about herself. "I'm no one."

"Madam Lenore raised her," Andre added.

The princess turned a skeptical glance in his direction before turning back to Elice. "Why would Madam Lenore raise a child?" Alice wrinkled her nose. "She's so ... old."

"Exactly what I was thinking," mused Andre. "But here's the crazy part: not only do you two look alike, you share a birthday."

Once again, the princess looked at the young man, her eyes wide as she took in the information.

Elice, feeling the weight of the words hanging heavily in the air, spoke before either of them could say anything else. "I'm sure it's just a coincidence. Lots of people share a birthday, right?"

The sound of the doors opening broke through the room, silencing whatever Andre was going to say next. In walked a woman; her floor-length silken green gown swayed with the movement of her steps as she sauntered into the room. Elice's breath hitched in her throat as she took in the sight of this elegant woman. The woman's dark brown curls bounced as she walked, a few strands of gray shining through her luxurious hair. She had a light brown skin tone and wore a simple silver crown over her head. A small smile adorned her face as she walked into the room, her gaze focused on Andre and Alice.

Elice forgot to breathe. The woman before her was breathtaking. However, even if she weren't, Elice was sure she would have had the same reaction. She was the spitting image of the woman before her; the only difference being Elice had darker skin.

"Lord Copita, I'm so happy you brought your cousin to visit," the woman said. Her smile vanished and she let out a small gasp as she looked at Elice.

Elice didn't know what to say. She stood there, looking as dumbfounded as she felt.

Without another word, the queen closed the remaining distance between them and wrapped Elice in her arms. With her arms trapped and hanging between their bodies, Elice froze in place. She didn't know why this woman was hugging her or—she assumed because of the queen's shaking shoulders—crying into her hair.

"You're here," she heard the woman say in between a sob. Elice tried to pull away, but the queen squeezed her into a tighter hug. After another moment, the woman pulled back to peer at Elice. Her eyes were glossy, and the remnants of tears streaked down her cheeks. She placed her hands on the sides of Elice's face and whispered, "Elice, you finally came back."

Elice meant to ask the woman how she knew her name. She wanted to ask what was going on. Instead, she stood there, mouth agape, unsure where her own voice had disappeared to because she no longer knew how to speak. She looked at Andre, and he shook his head at her, letting her know he didn't understand what was happening, either.

Then she looked at Alice—her mouth also hung open as she stared at the queen. When Elice returned her gaze to the queen, she realized the woman was studying her features. A frown was on her face, though, and her eyes quivered as if on the verge of more tears.

The woman lowered her hands from Elice's cheeks. "Surely you know who I am." Her voice was just above a whisper.

"You're the queen," answered Elice, shocked to hear her voice had returned.

"But Madam Lenore told you about me, other than me being the queen?"

Elice shook her head in response. It never occurred to her before how Lenore never talked about the royal family. It had also never occurred to her to ask about them, since she was nothing but an abomination to the kingdom with her uncontrollable powers.

Queen Julice's eyebrows furrowed, and the corners of her mouth turned down. She looked at the princess and then Elice before drawing in a deep breath. "Well, you must have mastered it by now, which is what she promised to teach you." The queen took a step away and stood with her back straight.

"Mastered ... what?" Elice said, feeling as if she missed something.

"Your magic. She promised to teach you how to control it so you could return. And now you're back." She placed gentle hands on each of Elice's shoulders, another tiny smile replacing her frown.

Elice took a step out of the woman's reach. She feared what would happen if she admitted she couldn't control her powers. However, she felt inclined to answer, wanting to get to the bottom of whatever was happening. "I can't control my magic." The queen's eyebrows furrowed, but Elice continued. "How do you know so much about me? How do you know anything about me at all?"

New tears streamed down the queen's face, falling to the soaked shoulder of her elegant gown. Her voice trembled when she spoke. "Because I'm your mother, of course."

She heard the princess's sharp inhale. Rather than focus on the sound, she gave her attention to the woman before her, trying to read through the words and the tears. Elice shook her head, not sure if she was trying to say no or shake away the thoughts that swam in there.

"There was a prophesy," the woman continued. Elice almost couldn't hear her over the sound of her own heart pounding. "It was after the war, after your father defeated Orser, the leader of the rebellion. We were all fearful of magic, but Madam Lenore insisted on giving a reading. She came to the castle completely unannounced—I was already over six months pregnant. She touched my belly to read the future of our unborn child, just like they did in the old days.

"First, she told us we were expecting twins, two daughters. I thought your father would faint. She said the firstborn would be a kind and loyal child, always putting the kingdom first. Then, she said the second-born would have magic, strong and dangerous powers that would rival Orser's."

Elice thought back to the times she witnessed Lenore having visions. She would pause, her eyes becoming distant as if she was watching something interesting take place in the air. Then, with a shudder, her vision would end, and she would return to whatever she was doing. Elice always asked what her visions were about, but the old mage would either ignore her questions or tell her she didn't need to know.

Queen Julice drew in another shaky breath. "We were so scared, so young. We didn't know what to do. She promised she would take you and train you to control your powers. She said she would bring you back to us as soon as you were ready. As time went on, we lost faith in her and demanded weekly updates. Then the updates came every month, then once a year. But we never imagined she was lying to us all along and that she had no intention of helping you—or that she would never tell you about us, about your family."

The queen never took her eyes off Elice. There was a hard-to-read expression in them, an ache that Elice had never seen before and couldn't place a name to. Was it sadness? Regret? She never saw this countenance on Lenore's wrinkled face.

An angry heat spread across her face and down into her chest. She could hear the princess sniffling beside her, but she faced the queen and forced away the fierce tears that threatened to escape. She never cried—Lenore would never let her.

"How could you?" she asked, her voice on the verge of breaking down and hiding again. "How could you give your own daughter away? Especially to that..." Elice didn't know how to continue, how to describe the woman who raised her. She thought about the loneliness, the pain of never feeling genuine love from the only person she ever knew.

Her resentment hardened as she looked at Alice—the young girl who was the epitome of everything Elice was not. She was graceful, quiet, and carried herself with elegance even as tears poured from her eyes. Elice imagined this girl receiving enormous amounts of love and attention from the moment she was born, while Elice had only ever known bitter words and icy glares.

"I didn't think..." The queen started, but stopped as a water droplet fell from above and landed on her forehead. It began as tiny dribbles, one after the other, but soon the drops grew bigger as they merged.

Elice could feel herself losing control. Her insides raged like a violent storm at sea, drawing up the surrounding moisture and letting it loose. The water called to her, gathering around her body in response to her swell of emotions.

Julice met her eyes, and they trembled with fear as she stared at her. Elice looked around the room and saw the same look reflected on Alice's and Andre's faces as well.

The rain she created was on the verge of picking up. Just like the time she flooded the tiny cottage, almost drowning Lenore in the process.

With as much willpower as she could muster, she closed her eyes and emptied her thoughts of emotion, just as Lenore had taught her. In the past, she needed several minutes to calm herself enough to control her powers. This time, however, she felt the tension and sadness dissipate quicker than ever before.

After several calming breaths, the water molecules she had held on to dispersed in the air. When she opened her eyes, the storm clouds she made had disappeared, and so had Queen Julice.

Elice began pacing the room again, her thoughts racing over everything that had happened. She thought about the old seer, how she needed to find her so she could hear what Lenore had to say. She wanted to know—*had* to know—if there was a reason for her lies. Why did the old woman say her parents were dead? Why had she never told her about her family? If Elice knew about them, perhaps she would have trained harder, focused more on controlling her magic so she could reunite with them.

She had forgotten about Andre and Alice, so she paused for a moment to look over at them. He held Alice in his arms as the princess buried her face against his chest. Elice couldn't bring herself to worry about them, though. She knew she had to leave, to continue what she had set out to do.

She had to find Lenore.

With a quick turn, she faced the door, determined to leave High-more castle as soon as possible.

"Wait," Alice called out. Elice paused, her hand in midair as she reached for the handle. "Please, wait."

Elice looked over her shoulder. "I have to go," she said, the harsh tone causing Alice to flinch. Tears glistened in the princess's eyes, and Elice's heart softened from the previous bitterness she felt toward her. It wasn't Alice's fault—they were both victims in all of this.

"I've always wanted a sister," Alice whispered, an uncertain smile on her lips.

An incredulous sound made its way out of Elice's mouth. "Me too, actually," she responded and stepped away from the door. She pulled at a strand of hair, the ringlet going straight until she let it go and it bounced up again.

Alice stepped forward as well until the two girls were an arm's length away. Andre, who stood to the side, cleared his throat.

"Well," he began, "as fun as this was, I believe you two have plenty of talking to do. You can thank me for my services to the crown at a later time." His lips curled into a playful smile, and he gave an exaggerated bow before leaving the room.

Elice stared at the closed door for a moment before returning her gaze to Alice, just as Alice turned to look at her. They smiled before they reached forward and pulled each other in for a hug.

Six

When they pulled away, Elice looked into the princess's eyes—her sister's eyes. She never thought about having a sibling, much less a twin. Madam Lenore only ever told her that her parents were casualties of the nearly three-decade-long war between Orser and the kingdom. Her questions about her parents always went unanswered. It frustrated her to no end, but as she grew older, she became used to Lenore's habit of sharing only what was necessary—which was not a lot.

Alice took both of Elice's hands and brought them close. "If I had known about you, I would have tried to find you. I would have asked to see you every day until our parents got sick of hearing me whine and brought you home."

Elice squeezed her sister's hand. "Thank you, but I don't think that would've worked. Something else is happening here, and I need to find out what it is."

Her twin pursed her lips and nodded her head. "Can I show you something first?"

She nodded, and before she knew it, Alice pulled her out of the room and down the lengthy hall. The walls were painted a bright white, and the floors were lined with thick, red carpet. They walked past a few closed doors, turned a corner, and continued down another long hallway. Elice knew she could get lost inside of the castle, being as large as it was.

She also knew that had she grown up inside its colossal walls, she would have learned her way around. She fought the sorrow and anger that popped up inside her at the thought of how much she had missed.

Alice stopped outside a door at the end of the hall. The princess gave a shy smile before she turned and opened the door, leading Elice into the room. Inside, dozens of paintings hung on every surface of the walls. There were also several tables, all of them covered with stacks of similar pieces of artwork.

Elice stood in the center of the room and turned in a full circle, taking in all the art surrounding her. One wall had a floor-to-ceiling glass door that led out to a patio and was framed by thick yellow curtains. The door was propped open, and a cool breeze swept in, greeting Elice as she spun around.

"Did you paint all these?" Elice looked at Alice, who still stood by the door.

Alice nodded in confirmation and stepped into the room, her arms folded in front of her. "This is my art room. I spend most of my time in here or on the patio working on my projects."

Elice acknowledged her with a nod of her own as she browsed

through the artwork on the closest table. There were several pieces, but the majority were of the same flower in various shades of red, as if she couldn't find the exact color she wanted. She stopped in front of a self-portrait, this one not yet complete.

She surveyed her sister's portrait, noticing the different style she used in this one compared to the one in Andre's estate. The beginnings of a hairstyle framed a complete face. Elice scrunched her eyes as she leaned in close, then jumped back as she realized it wasn't a self-portrait at all.

"Is that me?" she asked. Alice stepped forward to look at the painting in question. There were subtle differences only the two of them would notice—the color of the hair and skin, the long curls, the curve of the smile. These differences added up to one conclusion: the girl in this portrait was not Alice; it was Elice.

Alice hummed as she inspected her own work. "I didn't notice before, but now I see how this looks more like you than me." She walked to a nearby table along the wall and rummaged through the canvases. With another hum, she went to the next table and began searching again. "Ah, found it," she said, holding a fully painted canvas.

She walked away to a nearby stool, and Elice followed, sitting on the edge of the table beside her.

"I painted another one several months ago." Alice's voice was just above a whisper. Elice wondered if she was always this quiet.

She looked over Alice's shoulder and, sure enough, the painting in her hands looked more like Elice than Alice. "How did you do that? Are you a seer?"

"I don't know. I just paint what I see in my dreams. I wake up from such vivid dreams and I have a sudden urge to just … paint."

Elice tilted her head to the side as she thought about what this could mean. Was Alice having dreams, or visions, about her? If so, how was that possible? Elice had never heard of people having the ability to have visions while dreaming—usually they happened while the sight mage was awake or fully conscious. Then again, Lenore never explained much about visions, so there could be a lot she didn't know.

"Alice, I need to find Lenore. I need to know why she lied to me and to our parents."

The door to the art studio opened. At the doorway stood a man with short brown hair and a matching beard covering most of his face. He wore a lofty gold crown with several shiny diamonds encrusted throughout the spikes. He was imposing—tall and stately, wearing a cobalt blue cape that reached to the floor over a black button-up shirt and trousers. Elice knew who stood in front of her before he even spoke.

The king stepped forward into the room. His dark eyes shone with a deep and intense glint. "By the Fates, it really is you."

Elice glanced at her sister, who held the painting tight against her chest.

He cleared his throat and walked to the center of the room, standing with his hands behind his back. "Your mother told me that our reunion is not going as planned."

Elice could feel the frustration building up again. "I'm sure you can understand why."

The king turned toward the patio to stare outside. "Your mother and I did what we thought was best."

"Best for who?" She crossed her arms and attempted to steady her breathing.

"I had to consider how your powers would affect the entire kingdom."

"And what about me? Did you ever think how it would affect me?" Her fingers dug into her palms as she balled her hands into fists. She could feel the years of neglect, of being treated like a curse, advancing like bile rising in her throat.

The king continued to gaze outside, averting his attention, Elice noted with narrowed eyes. When he turned to her, he had set his expression to stone. "I am the king. The decisions I make benefit the commonwealth, not the individual. They are not to be questioned or challenged." Edgar stepped away from the patio door, passing a silent Alice on his way to stand in front of Elice. "We didn't know how strong you would be, only that your powers would rival those of Orser. I needed to ensure the safety of my people."

A raging fire rose inside Elice's belly as she stood from the table. It took all her effort not to summon magic, even though all she wanted to do was flood the room. "I have to get out of here. I have to find Lenore." She could no longer stay in the presence of this man—even if he was her father. If she heard his excuses any longer, she would have to work harder to contain her magic—which also meant it would expel stronger from her body when it finally released. She needed to leave this place right now.

"You cannot leave," he told her. "Since you still haven't gained control of your magic, you are a danger to those around you. It wouldn't be safe for you to leave the castle."

"All you care about is everyone else but me!" she screamed, not caring that he was a king and her father.

"I have a duty to the people!" He screamed as well; his nostrils flared, and his jaw clenched.

"Well, I don't care about the people! I need to find Lenore." She couldn't contain it any longer. A large gust of wind flew in from the door and gathered in her palms. The room filled with the swirling force of air as she released it.

Her hair covered her face as it whirled around with the surge of air. She could see her father's shocked expression through the gaps of her locks as he took several hurried steps away from her. His mouth hung open for a moment, but then he snapped it shut and halted his retreat. He glared at her, the sternness in his eyes boring a hole into her own.

Elice drew in a deep breath. "I'm sorry," she said, lowering her voice and the air, molecule by molecule, until the air stilled. "I don't want to hurt anyone."

She pushed her way past the king and stormed down the hallway. She took a left at the end of the hall, fighting tears and her powers as she stomped blindly along the corridor. She took a right and ran straight into a dead end. It continued this way for several minutes as Elice made many wrong turns until she finally found herself in the main entryway of the castle.

After bursting through the front doors, she ran across the concrete path toward the gate. When she approached, she saw Andre standing next to the guards. To her surprise, the gates were closed, and the men stood in front, barring both exit and entry of the castle grounds.

"Hey," Andre said once she came to a stop, "what happened?"

"This was a mistake," she said in a quivering voice. "I shouldn't have come here. I should've gone to find Lenore. I should've gone home. I should've..."

He placed a hand on her arm, his usual smile absent as his face took on a serious expression. "What went wrong?"

She shook her head and noticed her body shake with it as she tried to rein in her magic. She couldn't erupt, not out here where so many could see her. "They're afraid of me. They didn't want me. Even the woman who raised me lied to me."

"Madam Lenore has lied to everyone, I'm sure." His lips curved into a slight smile as he consoled her. "Besides, you can't trust that crazy old woman. Your parents are victims just as much as you are."

"I can't trust them, either. I have to leave. Otherwise I'll never find Lenore or the reason she did all this."

"You can't leave, I'm afraid." He scratched behind his ear and looked toward the guards. "That's why I'm here. I came to inform the guards to close the gates. The King has ordered a lockdown of the castle."

Elice narrowed her eyes. Was her father trying to keep her here? She turned and saw the king standing at the top of the steps leading into the castle. Her eyes thinned further as he glowered at her with his hands on his hips. She stomped toward him, Andre following close behind. As she drew closer to the entrance, Edgar turned and walked inside as if he expected her to follow.

Elice continued in his footsteps while thinking about what she would do next. Would she yell at him again? The boiling anger deep inside her gut told her she might. Would she demand he let her go? Even if she did, would he even let her? She heard what he had said—he thought she was a threat, and he valued the citizens more than her, more than her wants and needs. Even if she could prove she wasn't dangerous, which she couldn't, would he believe her enough to allow her to walk out of the gates?

He led her through the main foyer and into a large room just off the main hall. Elice scanned the room quickly—a large throne sat on a raised platform at the back of the space. It had intricate swirls etched across the wooden legs and a deep crimson cushion atop which the king sat.

Her eyes set on her father in the center of his throne room as she advanced toward him. "Why can't I leave?"

Edgar placed his arms on the armrests of his throne. "I've already told you. You're too dangerous."

"You don't know anything about my powers." She stood before him, fists clenched and heat surging through every pore. The anger threatened to boil over, and it took everything in her to keep from lashing out with a burst of magic.

"Then tell me: can you stop yourself from using magic?" He laced his fingers and leaned forward. "Can you control it enough not to use it?"

Elice wanted to tell him she was trying—yet she could feel light gusts of wind rushing between her fingers, pushing the air in the room. She could feel the ground beneath the stone floor, the roots and dirt begging her to call them forth. Even the tiny water molecules interspersed throughout the surrounding air asked to take form in her hands.

She sighed. "My powers are too strong. Even now, I can feel

them. But I can learn to control them if I keep trying."

King Edgar held up his hand to stop her from speaking. "That is proof enough. The use of magic is forbidden. I created this law to keep the citizens safe. If you use your magic, you'll be forced to face the consequences of breaking the law."

Elice balled her fists at his threat. "You've already locked me away my entire life. What more can you do?"

"I will do what I must for the good of the people." He stood from his throne to tower over her.

"I don't care about the people. I don't have a duty to them, and it's your fault for that."

"Enough of this! You are not leaving this castle." With his hands balled, he jumped from his seat and stormed out of the room. She followed him with her eyes as he left, reminding herself to take deep breaths before she exploded.

Alice stood in the open doorway. As if on cue, she walked up to Elice, grabbed her hand, and led her out of the room. They passed Andre on their way out. Elice knew he'd heard everything, even though he smiled at the two girls as they passed.

Elice trudged beside a quiet Alice. Neither one spoke a word—afraid to break the silence. Elice barely noticed the red carpet that lined this hallway and the array of closed doors along the way.

They stopped in front of a door that had been painted a pale white. Alice pointed to another one down the hall—it was much more elegant, with ornate flower designs etched across the surface. "That's my room," she said before turning to the one in front of them. "This one has been empty for as long as I can remember.

Mother refuses to allow anyone to sleep in it. Now I understand why. I think she was saving it for you."

Alice pushed open the door, and the hinges squeaked from the years of neglect. At first, Elice couldn't see anything—the massive window coverings darkened the room. Alice walked to the window and drew the curtains open. Both girls blinked, allowing their pupils to adjust to the sudden brightness.

"This is the parlor," Alice began. In the center sat two brown wing-backed chairs opposite each other, a short sofa along one wall, and a low table in the center. She pulled Elice past the sitting area to another door straight ahead that opened to a bedroom. "There's a bed, a dresser, and a wardrobe. We can order personal items for you, like bedding or furniture. Oh! There's a fabulous dressmaker in the town, though we'll have to summon her for a custom fitting since you can't..." Alice bit her lip to avoid finishing her sentence, but Elice already knew what she would say.

It hit her all at once, like a gust of wind on a stormy day. She was a prisoner—she went from hiding in a cramped cottage to being locked in a colossal castle. The talk of furniture and clothing did nothing to disguise the fact that she still had no free will. Elice had to remain where here until the day came when she could control her magic.

She wondered if that was a possibility. Could she learn to contain her powers? Would everyone always treat her like an abomination, no better than a common criminal who deserved nothing but to be sealed away, padlock and all?

Elice didn't realize she was crying until Alice's graceful arms wrapped around her shoulders. The sobs came next, her body jerking as she hid her face against her sister's shoulder. When she imagined life outside her cottage, this wasn't it.

Alice held her that way the entire time without complaint, and all Elice could do was wonder what she would do next.

Seven

Favorite color?"

"Yellow, of course," Alice answered and gestured to her lemon-colored dress.

Elice laughed—between Alice's current outfit and the self-portrait hanging in Andre's sitting room, she wouldn't have guessed otherwise. It was a bright color that reminded her more of wildflowers than the peaceful girl sitting before her on the bed. She thought about Andre's boisterous personality clashing with Alice's docile nature. She couldn't see how the two of them became engaged.

"What's your favorite hobby?" Alice asked. They had spent the past few hours taking turns asking each other questions. So far, they found that other than their facial features, they didn't really have much in common.

"Reading," Elice answered with ease. "I always get lost in books, no matter what they're about. It helped me not feel so lonely." Saying it aloud made her heart clench.

Alice hummed in agreement. "That's why I paint. Even when I'm surrounded by people, I always feel alone. To be honest, I would prefer to be alone. But when I'm painting, I get to enter a new world of my own creation."

Elice loved the way her sister's face lit up. "Maybe the Fates were trying to tell us we were missing something important in our lives."

"And now we have each other."

Elice gave her a smile and reached for her hand.

She wondered why the Fates hadn't brought them together sooner if they were both so lonesome. Perhaps their destiny was to go through childhood without each other so they could appreciate one another better in adulthood. It was a gut-wrenching thought, knowing their birthday was just over one week away, and in another year they would turn eighteen. They had missed out on so much of each other's lives. Elice wanted to find Lenore, but at least she had found the twin she never knew she had.

"What about your favorite food?" Alice asked, taking Elice's turn. Elice didn't realize she was so deep in her thoughts.

"I don't know, really. I had a garden with some fruits and vegetables, and I caught small game in the traps by the cottage. Lenore would bring flour and other things we couldn't grow."

"Then we must eat my favorite dish for dinner. I'll find a servant to make the request right away." Alice stood from the bed. "And I'll send someone in to help you dress for dinner." She patted Elice on the arm before she turned and left the bedroom.

Now that she was alone with her thoughts, her mind replayed

the events of the past two days. She wondered how long the king would keep her here against her will when she heard a knock on the door.

"Um... Come in?"

A tiny girl poked her head through the open door and curtseyed before she entered. She wore the same brown dress as the servant Elice saw earlier in the day, and she wore her hair pulled back in tight braids behind her head. Her arms were full of clothes that seemed much too heavy for her to carry since she was out of breath when she spoke. "Good evening, my lady. Princess Alice sent me to help you dress for dinner."

The young girl laid the gowns across the bed, then stood to the side, waiting for Elice to choose. All the dresses looked way too elegant for Elice's taste, as they were covered with embroidery and lace. She wondered if she could wear a simple outfit—one less frilly. Then she reminded herself these were likely Alice's clothes, and Alice was a princess. Which meant Elice was a princess, too.

She backed away from the bed like it was on fire. This was her new life—with a new mother, father, and sister—and this was who they wanted her to be. Was she now expected to go to balls? Was she supposed to speak formally and know all the laws of the land? Was she ever going to get out of this castle?

"My lady?" The servant furrowed her eyebrows in concern.

"I'm fine," Elice croaked out.

"Dinner will be ready shortly."

Elice heard the urgency in the girl's voice, warning her she needed to hurry. She pointed to a short-sleeved teal dress with white lace on the trims of the arms and skirt. It was the safest choice among the three, since the others had more embellishments. She reached for the dress, but the girl grabbed it first.

"I can put it on myself." Elice looked at the new dress, noting how the fabric seemed lighter than the one she borrowed from Andre's house. It lacked the many layers of skirts underneath and seemed easier to get into.

"But Princess Alice sent me to help you," the servant said, her eyebrows still wrinkled.

"Trust me. I've been dressing myself all my life. I can handle it." Elice pulled the dress away from the servant with a small smile. The girl continued to frown at her.

Elice turned around and began shimmying out of the bulky blue dress. Lenore's necklace swayed around her neck along with her movements. It took a few extra shakes than Elice originally planned for, but she managed to squeeze out of it. She then slipped into the soft teal dress. It surprised her how much she loved the feeling of the delicate, buttery fabric over her skin. She once again tucked the charm inside the bosom of her dress, hoping to conceal it as much as possible.

When she turned to face the maid again, the other girl motioned to a dainty white chair in front of a vanity. Elice gave a mental groan, but sat down and let the girl work through her long, chaotic curls.

"Can you at least tell me your name?" Elice asked through gritted teeth. The curls had tangled throughout the day, and the servant pulled a comb through a large knot.

"Me?" The girl met her eyes in the mirror before looking down at her task. "Oh, I'm Serena."

"Serena. That's a beautiful name."

Their eyes met again, and the young girl smiled. "Thank you. I'm named after my grandmother."

"That's so nice." Elice smiled at her. "My name's Elice."

The girl smiled again before continuing to pull at Elice's hair. Serena gathered Elice's thick hair and began piling it at the top of her head. With one hand, she reached into her pocket and pulled out a few hairpins. One by one, she stuck the pins into Elice's hair until all of it sat high in a tight bun. Elice blinked at herself in the mirror's reflection—she didn't recognize herself at all. "Um..."

"You don't like it?" Serena's eyes widened in panic.

"It's not that... I'm just not used to it." Elice turned her head from side to side, attempting to see it from all angles.

There was a quick knock on the door before it opened. Alice walked in wearing a white dress with capped shoulders and pale-yellow stitching throughout the bodice. "Wow, Elice, you look amazing."

Elice grimaced. She felt ridiculous.

"What is it?" Alice stepped closer.

"I don't feel like myself." She returned her gaze to the mirror.

Alice bent down so they were both reflected in the looking glass. "You look just like the princess you are."

There was a gasp, and Elice turned to see the shocked expression on Serena's face. The girl lowered her gaze and gave another curtsey. "Your highness, I apologize. I didn't know."

"You mean you couldn't see the resemblance?" Elice smirked at the girl's distress.

Serena's eyes widened. "Are you two..."

"Twins!" Alice finished. Elice thought her sister had never smiled this widely before.

"By the Fates," Serena whispered, placing her right palm over her heart.

Alice turned to Elice. "Shall we let your hair down?"

With her smile relaxing into a pensive look, Alice worked to loosen her bun. Elice watched as Serena took a breath and returned to her hair as well, helping Alice set it in a half-up style similar to Alice's. Elice kept her mouth closed this time, though she would have preferred her hair to follow its own wild and natural tendencies.

Serena reached for the make-up kit on the vanity, but Elice pushed it out of the way.

"But—" Serena began.

"Nope," Elice cut her off. "I'm not wearing that. The hair and dress are enough for one night." She caught the girl's eyes in the mirror.

Serena curtseyed again before excusing herself from the room. When Elice stood, Alice reached for her hand and, together, they walked out of the bedroom.

"You'll sit across from me at the table," Alice said.

"I don't even know how to eat a proper meal," Elice explained. "I don't know which utensils to use, or where to place my hands, or even what to say. I know what I want to say, which would probably just make everyone upset."

Alice hooked their arms as they continued out of the suite and toward the dining hall. "Don't worry about it. Just do what I do—and perhaps refrain from saying anything." She patted Elice's arm as if to reassure her, but Elice did not feel encouraged.

She always had a hard time keeping her tongue, which usually got her in trouble with Lenore. Being in front of the people who had caused her troubles in the first place would not put her in a good mood. She wanted to lash out at them, to make them see how much pain they caused her by forcing her to live with that old woman. Her head spun from the conflicting feelings this whole situation brought about.

There was little she could do, aside from sneaking out of the castle. However, if she snuck out, she wouldn't know what to do next. She didn't know anyone, and she didn't have a clue where Lenore was.

Being quiet was going to be harder than Alice made it out to be.

Alice led her to a sitting room, well lit by gilded candelabras scattered around, some attached to walls and others atop side tables. Thick mauve curtains covered the windows, and couches the color of amethyst sat across from each other in the middle of the room, with matching pillows for every cushion.

Paintings adorned the walls, and Elice realized they were images of various landmarks across the kingdom—the mountain peaks of Emori, the Lowlands with Fort Aramu's massive fortifications, a glorious composition of the cove near Fort Anchor, and a scene of one of the fishing villages that dotted the entire west coast of Norraine.

She tore her eyes from the beautiful paintings to focus on the other people in the room. The king and queen sat together on one of the lush sofas. Julice's eyes swirled with emotion, and Edgar's lips pressed into tight lines. Andre stood by a long sideboard table with various bottles and glasses. He wore a broad smile, which made Elice's cheeks warm at the sight.

The king stood, bringing Elice's attention away from Andre. "Now that you two have joined us, we can head into the dining room." Edgar motioned for Julice to walk ahead of him, and he followed her through a side door.

"Come on," Alice urged when Elice didn't move.

They passed by Andre, who gave a nod of his head. "You both look incredibly beautiful tonight."

Alice smiled and held on to Elice's arm as they made their way into the other room. "He's a sweet talker, that one," she whispered. "Try not to pay him any mind."

Elice nodded. She made a mental note to ask Alice later if Andre spoke like that to everyone.

The dining room had a similar style to the sitting room—with purple drapes and accents matching the adjacent room. A table large enough to seat eight people was the primary focus, with three matching candelabras placed in a row along the center. Along one wall was a long table with countless serving trays and pitchers of drinks. Alice led her to a seat, and a servant pulled the chair out so she could sit. She tried to time her movements correctly but ended up sitting too soon and almost fell to the floor.

"My apologies, my lady," the server said, reaching out a hand to steady Elice.

"It's my fault. Here, let me pull the chair in." Elice pulled the chair closer to the table by herself.

His eyes widened, and he looked as if he didn't know whether he should reply or do his job and help push the chair in.

Elice heard a chuckle from the other side of the table. Andre stared at her with amusement in his eyes as he gave a soft laugh. "I think she can do it by herself."

The young man nodded and took a few steps away. He wiped the disoriented look from his face as he stood at attention beside the serving trays. Elice faced forward in her chair and bit her lip so she wouldn't say anything else.

Another server was at her side in the next moment and lowered a serving tray with crisp greens and vegetables. Elice looked around and saw other servants setting plates in front of everyone else—her mother sat to her left at one head, her father opposite on her right. Alice sat in front of her and close to their father, and Andre was at Alice's right. Alice caught her attention with a pointed look and whispered, "Follow me," before she lifted a fork and held it up.

Elice understood—she grabbed a similar fork and brought it to her plate. They all ate in silence, even though Elice noticed her parents' watchful eyes linger on her. She wondered if this was how they ate every meal. Sure, she was used to eating in silence, but it was because she ate alone. Now she sat with four other people, yet none of them spoke a word.

She could feel the awkward tension hanging around them like a dense fog. She wanted to reach her hands out and pull the moisture from the air with her powers.

The king cleared his throat and inclined his head toward Andre. "How are the new recruits, Lord Copita?" Apparently, he couldn't handle the lack of conversation either.

"Let's just say they're better than the ragtag bunch during the infamous Fisher's Revolt." Andre laughed at his own joke.

Even Elice smiled at his jest about the Battle of Brant. Thanks to Lenore, she had a book that highlighted every battle in Norraine's three-hundred-year history. Boring, if she was being honest, but at least it was something to help her pass the time.

"Indeed," Edgar chuckled. "Year 32 was a rough year for my ancestors."

"You mean Year 36," Elice cut in before she lifted a piece of crunchy lettuce to her mouth.

Forks stopped midway between plates and mouths, which hung wide open. All eyes turned to look at her, and Elice was caught with her own fork halfway to her mouth.

"I'm sure it was Year 32," Edgar said, shaking his head before taking another bite of his salad.

Elice put her fork down and took a sip of water before she recalled what she had read. "The Fisher's Revolt began the third month of Year 36, after a bitter winter. It was two years into King Martin's reign, which began in Year 34."

She watched the king's thick eyebrows furrow as he remained quiet in thought. Then his brows rose toward his hairline.

"Well," he began, a deep huff resonating from his throat. "I find myself mistaken. You're correct. It was Year 36."

"How did you know that?" asked Andre, leaning forward.

"I read a lot," she answered, shrugging her shoulders.

"I'm sure you would love to visit the library," her father said with an interesting shimmer in his eyes. "It has thousands of books collected over the many generations of our family. In fact, my father commissioned dozens of books during his lifetime."

Elice couldn't find the words to respond, so she nodded. Was he inviting her to visit the library as his daughter or as a prisoner? She pressed her lips together before the question forced its way out.

Eight

That night, she found herself unable to sleep again. At the rate she was going, she knew she would suffer from the lack of proper rest. After much tossing and turning in her much-too-soft bed—it lacked the lumps of her old thin mattress and reminded her she was no longer home in her run-down cottage—Elice threw the plush covers off her body and jumped out of bed.

With a destination in mind but neither map nor clue how to find it, she wandered through the many long and dark halls of the palace. Now that she was alone, she took in everything before her—the soft red carpet, the gold sconces holding dimly lit candles, the various paintings and portraits decorating the walls, the console tables holding small vases or other valuable ornaments. Everything she saw was splendid and spoke of the wealth her family had inherited throughout the centuries.

Lost in her thoughts, she almost bumped into a servant carrying two empty buckets. Muttering a quick apology, she made a mental note to step cautiously in case she ran into a night guard. The last thing she wanted was to be caught sneaking around the empty castle at night—her father would surely think she meant to escape. Her jaw clenched at the reminder of her imprisonment in her own castle.

She peeked through several unlocked doors until she found the room she was looking for. Lit by a few candles, the library was indeed large. It took up two floors with rows of shelves perfectly aligned in the middle of the first floor. A staircase in the back of the room led to the second floor, where shelves lined the perimeter walls, and a shiny golden rail was set along the outside edge that encircled the entire upper level.

If she judged by her own minuscule bookcase, she would guess this library had ten thousand books. Books packed each shelf of every bookcase. Elice wandered through every aisle, scanning the titles of the books as she passed. Some books had spines that were creased with age or overuse. Most were in such pristine condition she doubted whether anyone had ever touched them.

Elice ran her fingers along a shelf until a title caught her attention—*Kings and Queens: A Family History*, with no author listed. She pulled it out from its spot and noticed the cover was fading but beautifully decorated with an intricate tree, the branches of which spread out across the front.

When she opened it, the branches continued on the inside page. The topmost branch had a name etched across it: Alexander Moore, the first king of Norraine. The branch next to his had the name of his wife, Yolanda. Their branches twisted around each other, turning downward before they split into three smaller branches for their children, with each name transcribed.

She turned the page as she strolled to a nearby table. She sat on a bench and sank into the deep cushion.

A branch from the previous page snaked to the top of the new page, with the name of Alexander and Yolanda's oldest child written on it. It connected to his wife's branch and then split into smaller branches for their children. It continued this way for every eldest child that a king or queen had, sometimes skipping the oldest because of death or using a cousin's branch from a previous page if a ruler did not have a child.

Flipping through the book, she saw the names of her ancestors archived in the most beautiful way. She could tell when an author added new pages—the stitches from the yarn used to sew the new page into the book peeked through and differed from the previous thread. Elice found it stunning to see how much history her family had.

There was a new connection forging in her heart to her ancestors through the fabric of this codex. It warmed her spirit to see their names and brought a smile to her face.

When she reached the most recent page, she saw her father's name on top, along with her mother's. Beneath it, she saw only one split branch. Alice's name was the only child written on this page.

Her breath caught somewhere in her throat. She wasn't in the family history book, where every family member had their name listed—even the troubled ones, like King John's youngest daughter Karina, who attempted to murder her older siblings in order to claim the throne.

Of course she knew why her parents never had her name transcribed on a branch. They had tried to hide the fact that she existed. But knowing the truth and experiencing the effects of the truth are two different things. The former you can ignore and brush off with a waving hand; the latter shows no remorse as it engulfs you and swallows you whole until you have no choice but to acknowledge it.

At that moment, Elice bathed in it. The waves of reality came crashing down on her and dragged her into its depths. With it came the tears from her soul as the emotions from the past two days flooded her. Her shoulders shook as actual tears escaped her eyes until she was sobbing.

She felt the moisture grow in the air around her. It gathered until she felt the water drops fall on her head and arms, threatening to soak her if she didn't stop crying.

With shaky breaths, Elice attempted to steady herself before she created a downpour in this beautiful library and ruined all the books. She folded her arms on the table, buried her head in them, and closed her eyes as she repeated a calming mantra.

"I'm not a curse," she muttered into her arm. "I'm not a curse."

She didn't know how long she had stayed that way, submerged in the grief and pain of being treated like an abomination. When she blinked her eyes back to reality, she saw the early morning light peek its way beneath the thick curtains of the library.

She had fallen asleep sitting on the bench, with her arms underneath her head on the hard wooden table. Her body felt sore and heavy as stone from all her weeping. She pushed herself up to stand on weak legs, holding on to the family tree book as she toddled her way out of the library.

Of course, she didn't know where her room was—she had stumbled into the library by accident, and her exhausted mind couldn't function enough to find her way back to the wing of suites. She wandered the halls, hoping to run into a servant who could point her in the right direction.

It must have been early, she realized, since she only spotted a few guards posted at the end of the long hallways. In an attempt to avoid them, she made many turns and redirections, which caused her weary mind to feel even more lost.

Elice saw a familiar plain white door and realized she had made her way back to the proper wing. She reached for the doorknob belonging to her room—she squinted at it, realizing this was now her newest version of a prison cell—when someone down the hall called her name. Turning toward the sound, she saw Alice leaving her bedroom.

"I see you woke up early." Alice wore another short-sleeved dress, this one all white with a yellow sash tied around the waist.

Elice rubbed her tired eyes and tried to stifle a yawn. "Sorry. I actually fell asleep in the library." She lifted the book as proof.

Alice's eyes lit up. "The family tree!" She rubbed a finger along the cover, following the curves of the thick branches that spread along the surface. "I haven't seen this in ages. I was ten the last time mother brought it out of the library."

Elice passed the book to her. "You can take it. Apparently, I'm not important enough to be in there anyway, so I don't need to keep it." She hated the feeling of self-pity that seeped out of her mouth with those words, but her sleep-deprived mind couldn't stop thinking about the ache in her heart now that it had burst forth from her chest.

Alice looked at the book and frowned. Elice turned to her door and entered, with Alice following closely behind.

"Come down and have breakfast with me," Alice said in a light tone, trying to brighten Elice's dark mood.

Elice wanted to protest—the need to throw herself in the oversized bed to sleep called out to her—but the grumbling in her stomach declared otherwise. "Let me change first." She headed toward the adjoining bathroom, placed the necklace on the counter, and freshened up.

Wrapped in a fluffy towel, she emerged and went to the wardrobe to browse through the choices. She selected a light blue gown with only two layers of underskirts. This one wouldn't require help to get into and would feel lighter than the others in the growing heat of summer.

Alice hooked arms with her as they walked down the stairs. She explained on the way how she requests her meals through her maid right after waking up each morning. This morning she made a request for Elice as well, and it would be ready as soon as they arrive.

"So, you don't actually talk to the kitchen staff?" Elice didn't like to think her family treated the servants as unimportant. It reminded her of how she felt, and she refused to treat others that way.

"Why would I?" Alice asked, her calm expression portraying how little she understood the position Elice was in.

"Oh, I don't know," Elice sighed, unlocking her arm from her sister's. "Maybe because they deserve to be treated with a little respect. Do you even know their names?"

Alice opened her mouth, but then snapped it shut.

"See!" Elice rolled her eyes. "I'm sorry to say this, but it seems like you really don't care about these people." She wondered if her father was the same way, after all his talk about putting the citizens first. She felt inclined to test his level of respect for the citizens he claimed to care so much about.

They continued in silence. In the dining room, the servants had placed the table settings for two in the same spots she and Alice sat at last night. As soon as they sat, servants came in with two plates full of pastries, fried eggs, and fruit. Another came in right after, holding a tray with a pitcher of what looked like freshly squeezed lemon juice.

During their meal, Alice seemed deep in thought as they sat at the massive table. Once they finished their breakfast, Alice turned to her. "You're right," Alice declared as the servants cleared away the plates.

Elice looked up and waited for her to continue.

Alice took a deep breath. "If I'm to be queen, I need to remember that all citizens are worthy of respect. I've lived a sheltered life, but that's no excuse for treating people differently based on their status."

A rueful smile broke across Elice's lips. "I may have been too harsh on you. I only meant for you to see things from a different perspective."

"You spoke the truth. You made me think about this seriously.

No one's ever made me think about this sort of thing before."

Elice shrugged. "I guess I can see things from the servants' perspective. Living with Lenore must have caused me to feel this way."

"How so?"

"Well, I've done everything myself all my life. It's all I know. Now, here I am, being waited on and having things done for me... I guess I just know what it's like to be on the other side."

They stood and walked out of the dining room. Alice extended her hand for Elice's and asked, "Would you like a tour of the castle?" Alice's voice was hopeful, which made Elice smile.

"I could use one, since I'm expected to stay here now." She placed her hand in her sister's.

Alice led her through the halls, describing things as they passed and pointing out important rooms. On the first floor, Alice showed her the room in which they first met. The council room was next to the throne room, which happened to be the first room off the main foyer.

They walked inside, and Elice had the chance to take in the massive hall without her father looming from his chair in the center of the room. She noticed two smaller chairs that she missed the first time, one on either side. The light-gray stone floors reflected the light, making the room appear bright. Four white columns from the floor to the high vaulted ceiling shined in the early morning light from the open windows in the back of the hall. Looking up, two red banners with the king's golden crown hung from the ceiling behind the raised dais.

Elice walked to the throne and reached out a hand to touch it when she heard a cough. She looked to the side and saw a guard standing beside a column with his arms crossed. He didn't make eye contact, but Elice knew he coughed in warning to let her know the throne was off-limits.

"Come, Princess Elice, there's more to see," Alice said, eyeing the guard as she walked past him to stand beside Elice. Though his eyes remained focused ahead, his eyes widened a mere inch when he heard her name.

It continued this way for the rest of the morning as the two girls wandered the castle. Whenever they ran into someone, Alice would lift her chin in pride and introduce Elice as her sister. The halls were busy with servants bustling about now that the sun was higher in the sky.

Elice also noticed people dressed in formal attire, not the typical servant's uniform. Alice seemed to avoid talking with these people, but they each placed their hands over their chest as they saw Alice approaching.

They came upon an open doorway that led out to a patio. The warm summer air wrapped around Elice's skin, welcoming her outside. She let out a deep sigh of appreciation. This was what she needed—to feel the elements and be one with nature.

Alice stared at her with a curious smile. "You like being out-doors?"

"You could say that," Elice answered with a smirk. She knew she shouldn't say out loud how much being in nature comforted her and her powers. After all, she was supposed to learn how to control them, not fuel them.

Alice lowered her voice and pulled her past the patio. "I have something to show you."

They walked through the courtyard and into an open field behind the castle. There were several groups of people, many of whom were soldiers wearing a uniform similar to the one Andre wore. Alice continued to walk arm-in-arm with her until they entered a garden. There were tall oak trees on either side of a path that led to a pond. Elice peered into the water to find small fish swimming along the bottom of the tiny reservoir.

There was a break in the path on the left side of the pond. The dirt was hard packed as if frequently walked on. Alice led her through a small gap in the trees. The two girls ducked under low branches until they emerged in a small garden.

Elice's mouth dropped as she took in the sight before her. They were in the middle of a small enclosure, blocked on all four sides by thick, giant arbor trees. Beautiful flowers of every color bloomed in their beds, framing the square space. The only furniture was a small metal bench, a painting easel, and a stool in the middle of the garden.

"What is this place?" Elice asked, her voice coming out lighter than it had been over the past several days.

"This is my oasis," Alice answered, looking around the garden herself. "I come here often—when I want to get away from the commotion of palace life. Mother thought I needed a private space to just be myself. The quiet, the calm, the beauty..."

"It's just like you." Elice sat on the bench and inhaled the fresh scent that only nature could provide.

Alice blushed as she sat down next to her. "When I'm not in my study, I paint in this garden. Inspiration comes easier for me here."

"I can see why. It's so peaceful. But none of these flowers look anything like the ones you painted."

"I suppose not." Alice looked around. There were no red flowers in this garden. "I dream about it, I think. It's unclear when I wake up, which is why I struggle with the color."

"What kind of flower is it? I have—well, had a garden at the cottage, and I've never seen a flower like it. The petals you drew are so droopy."

Alice frowned and looked down at her hands. "I don't know."

They sat in silence for a long moment, enjoying the warmth of the weather, the scent of the evergreen trees, and freshly bloomed flowers. Suddenly, Alice reached over and grabbed Elice's hand.

"I just remembered something," she began, sounding hesitant and regretful.

Elice raised an inquiring eyebrow. "Should I be worried?"

Alice's mouth twitched at the corner. "Mother wants you to come with me to meet Miss Tabitha this afternoon." She paused, allowing the suspense to build.

"Who's Miss Tabitha?" By the look on her sister's face, Elice's apprehension grew.

"She's my governess."

"All right, so..."

Alice's hesitation was maddening to Elice's already frayed nerves. "This is the last month she'll be in charge of my education, since school is compulsory only until age seventeen. In celebration, she's planning my birthday party—now *our* birthday party."

Elice lifted her hands as if to stop Alice. "I don't want a birthday party."

Alice turned and held both of Elice's hands. "That part was my idea. I told mother last night after you went to bed that I think it would be nice to have a dual birthday party—to celebrate our first birthday together."

Elice bit her lip. She didn't want to be in the castle until her birthday—that was eight days away. Yet, she still had no escape plan and no way of finding Lenore even if she escaped.

She sighed and nodded her head. "All right, we can have a dual birthday party."

Alice smiled a gentle, genuine smile. "It will be the best birthday party I've ever had."

Elice grinned in reply. "It will be the only birthday party I've ever had."

∿

"So, the rumors are true."

Elice narrowed her eyes at the woman in front of her. She was tall and curvy, and her black and brown spotted hair wrap sat in a perfect bundle atop her head. She wore an ankle-length black dress, which hugged every curve without modesty. Her fingernails had a coat of red paint, and her shoes were shiny black. They had the tallest heel Elice had ever seen, considering she owned only one pair of shoes all her life.

Then her eyes softened—she appreciated the woman's unique sense of style in a castle where everyone seemed to either wear floor-length ball gowns or uniforms.

"I heard we had a new guest in the castle this morning," Miss Tabitha continued, "but I didn't believe the maids when they said she was the long-lost princess."

Long-lost princess? Elice gave an incredulous snort, and Miss Tabitha raised an eyebrow at her.

Alice cleared her throat. "This is my sister, Elice of House Moore, Princess of Norraine."

Elice's heart drummed in her chest. Alice met her eyes and gave an encouraging smile. This was the first time she heard her full title, and she wondered if this was how she was going to be introduced from here on.

"Well," Miss Tabitha nodded, looking back and forth between the two sisters. "You two must be twins. Which means the rumor of an illegitimate child is incorrect." The woman ignored the girls' shocked expressions as she spun on her fabulous heels and hooked them both by the elbows, guiding them toward a table. "Come, Princess Elice, you must tell me where you have been hiding all these years."

Thankfully, in the garden, they had prepared a response to this kind of question. Alice turned her head toward the woman. "Princess Elice received private schooling and has been living with relatives in the Lowlands. Now that we are turning seventeen, she's come home to live in the castle."

"Ah, the Lowlands." Miss Tabitha nodded as they all sat around the four-seat table in her office. "How is Fort Aramu? In all my travels, I have yet to see that monumental citadel. My family is from the west, near the town of Anchor. As much as I loved living near the coast, I can't bring myself to head south toward the Swamplands. No amount of water and sunshine can prepare me for the humidity of the south."

Elice's mind whirled as she tried to recall what she had read about the great Fort Aramu. "It's very humid, but the citadel itself is a refuge. The River of Might runs through the city, and there's the Mighty Lake, so there's enough fresh water for drinking and farming. Besides, the fort is a few miles away from the swamplands—it's not as muggy as you might think."

"I might visit one day, then!" Miss Tabitha clapped her slender hands together once and then slid a pile of papers across the table. "I have to meet with the florist soon, so let's get to the party-planning."

The twins shared a relieved glance at having avoided further conversation about Elice's previous whereabouts.

Miss Tabitha pulled a notebook from the middle of the table. She spent the first few minutes informing Elice where things stood with the party.

Elice looked down at the sheets of paper—there was an extensive guest list of over three hundred people; a music list for a live orchestra; and a full menu with appetizers, a main course, desserts, and snacks to last throughout the night. Not to mention the images of gowns, shoes, tableware, and other items Elice didn't think she would ever need to celebrate her birthday.

To Elice's horror, it was more than just a party.

She interrupted the woman by holding up a hand. "This is a formal ball."

"My dear," Miss Tabitha said, giving a quick chuckle. "How else would you celebrate your birthday?"

"I don't know," she answered, looking to Alice for help. Alice only stared at her. "Does it have to be so ... excessive?"

The governess laughed again. "Didn't they have balls at the Great Fort? Just as I told Princess Alice, you need to make a statement."

"What does that mean?"

The woman took a deep breath. "You will finally be introduced to high society. No one knows who you are, which means everyone thinks they know who you are. The rumors will only spread until we show them who Princess Elice is. A ball is the perfect opportunity to do that, with all the nobles dancing about and vying for your attention. Not to mention the date on your arm—"

Elice cut her off. "Date?"

Miss Tabitha raised an eyebrow. "Of course, Princess. You must have a date."

"I don't need a date to go to my own birthday party."

This time, Alice spoke up. "Actually, it's tradition. Our escorts will lead us onto the ballroom floor for the first dance of the night."

"Exactly!" Miss Tabitha said.

"You said nothing about dancing!" Elice's voice was shrill. She had never danced before, not to mention in front of three hundred people. Her heart pounded in her chest, overwhelmed by how unnerving the past few days had been.

"Come now, Your Highness, you don't need to be so worried. It's only a party."

"I don't even want this party!"

Miss Tabitha opened her mouth, but Elice stood and left the room before she could say anything.

Nine

By the time Elice looked up from her book, darkness had crept in through the open window. She set her book aside and closed it, pulling the drapes closed as well. Settling back on the cushioned bench in a hidden nook near the back of the library, she opened the book to continue reading.

By far, this was the most informative book she had ever read. Elice assumed her father had authorized its composition, as it was a first-hand account about the end of the Last Mage War, within the first year of his reign.

Most of what she read was a biography. It was all new information for her about her father—even about Orser, the fire mage who led the rebellion against the kingdom.

She picked up where she had left off.

It was a startling sight for King Edgar to behold. Madam Lenore stood before him, her long, dark hair in thick braids down the center of her back, and her face the picture of youth. She looked to be around twenty years old, but everyone knew the truth regarding the power of the Blood Flower of which she consumed.

"To what do I owe the pleasure, Lenore?" King Edgar asked. He sat upon his throne, his eyes flashing in challenge. Queen Julice, his new bride, sat on a matching throne to his right.

"It's Madam Lenore, as you well know, your highness," she responded, her eyes and tone of voice meeting the king's dare.

King Edgar straightened his back and raised his chin. "You come into my castle, after everything you and your consorts have done, and expect me to show you kindness? To show you respect?"

"Yes," Madam Lenore answered, her lips spreading into a sneer. "Especially when I come bearing gifts for the new couple."

"I should lock you up and have you sentenced to death for treason." At the king's words, the guards around the room took a step closer to the sight mage as if to arrest her.

"You don't want to do that. Not when I have valuable information for you that could end the war."

General Thiery looked to his king for instruction, his hand on the hilt of his sheathed sword. King Edgar held up a hand to steady his men, and they stopped their advance.

"Talk," he commanded, turning a glare on Madam Lenore.

"I can tell you where the Blood Flower is." Madam Lenore lowered her voice, making the king lean forward in his seat.

"Why would you do such a thing?" His eyes narrowed on the woman before him.

"Because I have seen the error of my ways."

King Edgar barked out a laugh. "Is that supposed to be a jest? Tell me—you had a vision, didn't you? You saw that I will win this war."

"I see many things, and one of them is how the war will end."

"Do I win?"

She held a hand to her heart in mock surprise. "My king, do you want a reading of your future?"

King Edgar narrowed his eyes again. "That won't be necessary. Tell me where the Blood Flower is."

"I will need something from you first."

"You think you can barter a trade? My father, my father's father, and his father before have all fallen to you. Now it is up to me to redeem their efforts, and I will ensure I avenge my ancestors."

"I did not kill your ancestors."

King Edgar scoffed. "My forefathers may not have died by your hands, but their blood is on them, nonetheless."

"I see now that Orser's goal is short-sighted. He means to remove non-mages from power, with little oversight into what will become of us afterward, other than him taking your throne."

"And you have seen your untimely end?"

"The vision I had was not of my side winning." She shifted her gaze to the side.

King Edgar grinned and leaned back in his seat. "So, now you know you have chosen the wrong side."

Madam Lenore pursed her lips. "I will not say I was wrong. I only go by what I see."

"Well, tell me what it is you want, and I will see if I can make it happen."

"I want immunity. As soon as you cut down the flower, all of its magical properties will rapidly drain. Of course, Orser will then be mortal, so you may finally kill him. But that means I will also be susceptible to death, and my true age will make it impossible for me to defend myself. The Fire Lords will surely come for me after learning I caused their downfall. I want your word that you will protect me from their wrath. And I want to be free from prosecution by the crown."

King Edgar sat in silence, the fingers of one hand cupping his chin as he thought over her words. After a long moment, he said, "I will grant you immunity on one condition: you will guide me to the Blood Flower tonight."

"It is done, then." Madam Lenore placed her hands, one over the other, above her heart and closed her eyes. King Edgar, however, did not miss the smirk that played on her lips as she bowed her head.

The library door opened, and she snapped her eyes up from the book. She took steadying breaths to calm her racing pulse as she tried to make sense of what she just read. The sound of heels knocking against the stone floors echoed down the aisle as someone called her name. She folded the page to mark her spot before closing the book.

She readied herself, knowing it was her mother's voice calling for her, yet not ready to talk to her. Even if Julice were to find her in a matter of moments, Elice wanted to drag the wait out as long as she could.

Her mother's footsteps grew louder as the woman moved down the hall. Finally, she appeared in front of the nook behind the last row of bookshelves.

"There you are," Julice said. Elice opened her mouth to say something, but snapped it shut when her mother held up a hand to silence her. "I understand we didn't get off to the right start. However, a birthday is an important day for a young girl, especially for a princess."

"I've only been a princess for two days," she cut in before the woman could continue, earning her a reproving stare.

Her mother sat next to her on the bench. "Be that as it may, you were born into royalty, therefore you must live up to the expectations of society."

"But I don't know the first thing about being a princess." She turned to look at Julice, wondering why the woman was talking to her about a party when she had banished her from society in the first place.

"I know you never learned proper decorum. Miss Tabitha will be more than happy to give you lessons before the big day."

"And if I refuse?" She knew the answer, but had to ask.

Julice sighed and shook her head. "You are nothing like your sister."

Elice wanted to remind her that Alice wasn't raised by an untrustworthy sight mage who lied to her all her life, but bit her lip to keep from saying it aloud.

"I'm still angry," she said instead. "I don't know how to forgive you or Father for sending me to live with Lenore. And I need you to respect that I can't let it go so soon."

Her mother nodded. "I don't expect all to be forgiven, as I have yet to forgive myself." Elice was sure her eyes went wide at her mother's confession, because Julice shook her head again and looked her in the eyes. "Surely you don't think of me as a monster without a heart. I didn't mean for any of this to happen. I only did what I thought was best."

Elice looked down at the book in her hands. Did Lenore see this far into the future? The old mage must have had an ulterior motive when she approached her parents to offer them a chance to end Orser.

She shuddered—it shocked her to find out after all this time that Lenore had fought in the war. Why had the woman never told Elice about her part in it? She thought about Lenore's words. What did she mean about being susceptible to death and her true age?

What was this Blood Flower her father seemed to want to destroy so badly?

Elice was reminded of the protection charm that rested on the counter in her bathroom. If Elice ever had the chance to speak with Lenore again, she would have so many questions for her. The thought of never seeing her again caused her eyes to water, no matter how terribly the woman had treated her.

"I see you found my book," Julice said, drawing Elice from her introspection.

Elice's mouth fell open. "You wrote this?"

The queen motioned for the book and, after Elice handed it to her, she began flipping through the pages. "I've written quite a few for our library. I could give you a list if you wish to peruse them." She handed the book back to Elice before standing up.

Julice turned to leave, then spun around again. "You will still attend the ball and have an escort. Miss Tabitha will expect you tomorrow at eight in the morning to prepare." With that, she continued down the hall.

The chill of the fresh night air wove its way across Elice's body, beseeching her to bend it to her will. Her fingers itched to use magic, to pull and twist the surrounding breeze into a new shape. She had to keep the urge at bay since she was no longer in her remote cabin. After two days of betrayal and its subsequent heartache, her body was a mess of tension. She needed to release her pent-up magical energy—otherwise, she might continue to explode with her words and her magic.

Avoiding the guards, Elice wandered the outer fields of the castle, glad it was so late at night that not a soul could be seen. She found her way to the soldiers' barracks, their dormitories and facilities a few feet in front of her. She thought about finding one of their training rooms when she caught sight of a lone shed just off the shoulder of the encampment. It seemed to be hidden from view, since it stood behind one of the larger buildings. The metal siding was rusted, so she assumed it was a seldom-used storage room.

This is the perfect place, she thought as she made her way inside.

The inside was cramped, with a crooked table, a few busted military helmets, and empty sacks taking up most of the space. However, she had just enough room to expel some of her magic.

In one corner of the space, she saw a figure in the shadows. After a few seconds, with no movement from the figure, she looked at the nearby table and found a candle and match. After she lit the candle, she crept toward the corner. As she reached the shadowy figure, she let go of the breath she held when she saw it was only a stuffed mannequin, one used by soldiers as a practice dummy during training. Smiling, she closed her eyes and let her grievances loose on the poor, unsuspecting dummy.

Elice called to the earth first. Through her powers, she felt pieces of rock mixed in with the dirt on the floor. She pulled at them in her mind and raised her arms. Ten rocks shot straight up, hovering in the air. Closing her eyes, she fired them directly at the dummy in the corner. She opened her eyes again as some of the gravel slammed against the dummy, while a couple with sharper edges sliced at its cloth covering.

Next, she reached for the air, gathering it into a large gust and pushing it toward the figure. She held on to her pose—her right leg bent in front of her body, the other angled behind, and her hands with the palms out. The wind continued to pound the dummy for several seconds until she dropped her hands.

She spun to the left, calling for the water droplets to accumulate in her cupped hands. Landing with her left leg in front this time, she pushed the water at the dummy with as much force as she could muster. The dummy slid to the ground, now soaked, but Elice had yet to reach her fill.

After an hour of pouring her chagrin on the practice mannequin, she finally felt appeased. The mannequin, however, was destroyed. Its cloth covering that made up the arms and head split open. The bits of hay and cotton stuffing laid in a jumbled, sopping mess on the floor. Pieces of roots that she had called forth from beneath the dirt stuck out of the dummy's chest like swords, impaling it from all sides.

She wiped her muddy hands on her blue dress, not caring that she looked filthy. Satisfied with her work, she felt as though she might actually sleep well.

Elice tip-toed through the empty halls, avoiding the corners she saw the guards in earlier. As she grew closer to her room, she heard the sounds of shoes advancing down the quiet hallway. Her breath hitched as she stopped walking, holding her breath to avoid making any noise.

The steps grew closer ahead of her in the hall, though the nearby candles only shed enough light for her to see a few feet ahead. She could only hear the approaching person, not see them.

As quietly as she could, she took a few steps backward in the direction she came. The corner she just rounded was only steps away. If she could make it to the corner, she might be able to hide without being caught by whoever was in front of her.

Elice placed her hand along the wall as she walked. Two more steps, and she felt the corner with her fingertips. With a jump, she turned and placed her back against the wall, making herself flat against its surface.

In a matter of seconds, the other person's footsteps sounded next to her on the other side of the wall. She closed her eyes, knowing if the person turned her way, she'd be caught and have to explain why she was wandering the halls so late. Her mind had a second to come up with a reasonable excuse, which she was not good at doing.

She heard the footfalls continue down the opposite hall as the person turned the other way from where she hid.

She let out a slow breath, afraid to make any noise in case the person was close enough to hear her sigh. After counting to thirty, she eased around the corner and hurried down the hallway as fast as she could. Once she reached her suite's door, she pushed it open and then shut it, leaving her arms extended against the wood to hold up her exhausted body. Her head fell forward to hang between her arms.

With her adrenaline still pumping, she turned and walked toward her bedroom. She changed out of her muddy dress and into a soft nightgown. It took several beats of her heart to calm down enough to crawl into bed. After sliding under the heavy covers, though, her eyes fell shut right away.

When she awoke the next morning, she felt better than she had the day before. Serena entered the room to help her change for the day, and she remembered her meeting with Miss Tabitha. With a groan, she shooed Serena out of the room, telling her she could bathe and dress herself.

At a quarter past eight, she waltzed her way into Miss Tabitha's office.

"I suppose they never taught you how to read a clock at Fort Aramu." Miss Tabitha sat at her desk and peered at her over a sheet of paper.

Elice pulled out a chair, dropped into it, and puffed out a breath. "I'm sorry I'm late. I overslept."

"Lesson one: always arrive on time for your engagements. Lesson two: a princess never apologizes. She should thank others for waiting patiently or somehow turn it around and have others apologize to her." Miss Tabitha grabbed a thick book from her desk and placed it in front of Elice.

"What's this?"

"Since I hear you love reading so much, you are going to read this manual on proper etiquette. A princess must always maintain manners, politeness, and civility."

"You want me to read this entire book?" Elice eyed the large tome. "It has to be five hundred pages thick."

"Then perhaps you should get to it, Princess. You only have seven days before the ball, and your parents expressed to me their expectation to teach you all this and more within that time." She clapped her hands in a bid for haste.

"All right!" Elice exclaimed, rushing to open the book before Miss Tabitha banged her hands again.

"I have a few other party matters to see to this morning. I shall return shortly." She stepped out of the room, leaving Elice to read the book on her own.

Elice glanced at the first page. In boring detail, it covered the definition of etiquette and its importance in high society. She turned the page and continued reading. Page after page, she learned the history of etiquette in Norraine, which stemmed from her people's origins on the main continent, in the kingdom of Newton. She had learned from the family tree book that her mother hailed from Newton, which meant that Elice's ancestors had so much history.

She stifled many yawns, knowing she needed to get more sleep, or she would always feel this exhausted. After several hours, Miss Tabitha returned to her office. "You've made some progress. Excellent." She strolled to the table and sat next to Elice.

Elice held her tongue in her mouth, biting back the sarcastic remark she wished to share. Miss Tabitha began quizzing her on the information she read until a knock on the door interrupted them.

"Enter," Miss Tabitha shouted, and in walked a young man. He wore a buttoned-down blue shirt and gray fitted trousers. "So good of you to join us. Please, come in." Miss Tabitha stood, grabbing Elice by the elbow to haul her up as well.

"Of course, Miss Tabitha," the young man said, bowing his head. Elice got a good look at him when he stepped into the room. He had a thick head of neatly trimmed hair and wore a gold watch on his wrist. He had an aura of wealth and bravado to him that made Elice purse her lips.

"Lord Mead, may I introduce you to Princess Elice of Moore, second daughter to King Edgar and Queen Julice." Miss Tabitha stepped aside to allow the man to introduce himself.

He placed a hand over his heart and bowed. "Princess Elice, it's a pleasure to meet you. My name is George Brook."

Elice nodded as the governess continued with the introduction. "He's here to meet with you, Princess. Why don't you two sit? I will have some tea brought in." Miss Tabitha's grin was bright as she ushered George to the table. When they sat, she left the room to call on a servant.

She returned right away and continued to play matchmaker. "Lord Mead, why don't you tell Princess Elice about your familial lands?"

"Yes," he answered, turning toward Elice. "The crown has endowed the Brook family with a large plot of land to the west of the River of Might."

"I know a bit about Mead," Elice said. "It's a large coastal city with lots of shipping docks."

"My ancestors helped build those docks, and we still manage them today."

"So," Miss Tabitha cut in, "the Brook family is very well off."

George smirked at Elice. "Very," he said, a sultry note playing in his tone of voice.

Elice couldn't hold back the grimace that washed over her face. From the way George's face fell, he noticed it too.

"But," he stammered, trying to avoid putting Elice off, "we give to the Orphaned Children's charity at least twice a year."

"That's wonderful," Miss Tabitha exclaimed. "Did you hear that, Princess Elice? They donate to charity."

She rolled her eyes at the show before her. If this was how Miss Tabitha was going to play, then she would make sure she played her part as well. *Let's see who has the last laugh*, she thought, and forced a yawn. The governess glared at her before turning to Lord Mead to probe for more opportunities to attract Elice's affections to him.

It continued that way for the rest of the day. Once Lord Mead left—he tried to kiss Elice's hand, but she yanked it away before he could get it to his lips—it was a nonstop ambush of potential suitors. She met the sons of many noble families from across the kingdom, and she had given each one of them a hard time.

By dinnertime, she had worn Miss Tabitha so thin, the woman's vibrant headscarf hung lopsidedly on her head, exposing the curly hair underneath.

"We must remain vigilant," she said with too much cheer. "Tomorrow is a new day, and there are a few more suitors to meet. Off you go, now, so I may close out my office for the day."

***

A smile remained plastered on Elice's face as she strode into the family's sitting room. Only Alice and Andre were there, sitting together on a couch. Elice sat across from them and breathed a sigh as she settled into the cushions.

"Long day?" Andre asked over his glass, and Elice could smell the alcohol drifting off him.

"Miss Tabitha had me meet a few suitors today, after I spent three hours of mindless reading from The Book of Proper Etiquette."

Andre laughed and took a sip from his drink.

Alice smiled. "I remember that book. I was five, maybe six, when I first had to read from it."

Elice looked at her sister with raised eyebrows. "You read it when you were five?"

"The previous governess thought I should start early."

"And she had us dancing around the ballroom at eight," Andre said.

"Please tell me that's not when you became engaged." Elice's eyebrows still threatened to reach for her hairline.

They shared a look with each other that made Elice wonder if they were having a silent conversation through their eye contact.

"Father wanted to ensure the advancement of the Moore line," Alice answered, her typical quiet tone just above a whisper. "He had us officially betrothed last year on my sixteenth birthday, but I suspect he planned it a long time before that."

"That's..." Elice paused. It was many things, horrible being number one.

"It is what it is," Andre finished for her. "Alice is my best friend, and I serve my king and country before myself."

She looked at the young couple before her as understanding dawned on her. They weren't in love with each other. The king had forced them into this engagement. He wanted Alice to be wed right away in case Elice turned out to be evil, so he could have at least one child's future secured. Their father had contained and restricted Alice's life so he could make sure the Moore legacy lived on. Regardless of how Elice turned out, he had amassed all his energy to seal Alice's fate.

"If you need a date to the party," Andre interrupted her thoughts with his jovial voice, "I know a subordinate on my squad who is the perfect gentleman. I can send him to meet you and Miss Tabitha tomorrow. He wouldn't mind serving as your placeholder."

Elice nodded at his suggestion, but it was hard to take his comment seriously when his eyes met hers with such fire. She could read the expression behind his buoyant facade, and it made her blush.

Andre may be engaged to Alice, but he wasn't in love with her. That meant his affections would always be at risk of straying elsewhere.

Ten

A bead of sweat rolled down her forehead, and she wiped it away with the back of her hand. Her thick curls, which were tied in a loose ponytail behind her head a few minutes earlier, skirted around her face.

When she first arrived in the abandoned shed behind the barracks that evening, she was shocked to find a new mannequin sitting in the same corner as the one she had destroyed the night before. It was a gift from the Fates, she thought, since she needed another outlet for her confusing life. After a thorough release of stress, there it lay, pummeled to a pulp by the onslaught of attacks she unleashed upon it.

Panting from the exertion, she turned around to take a break from her triumph over the cloth dummy and let out a startled gasp. Standing in the doorway to the shed was the silhouette of a person. He had been leaning against the doorframe, but when she jumped in alarm, he stood straight and stepped into the small room.

"I apologize," he said, his voice a deep whisper as it resonated in the small space. "I didn't mean to startle you."

Elice backed up a step toward the battered mannequin as an icy dread swept over her.

When she didn't respond, he spoke again. "I tried to stay quiet so I wouldn't disturb you. I just wanted to find out who destroyed my practice dummy."

He confirmed what she feared: he had seen her use magic. Would he tell the king? If he did, what would her father do? Elice did not want to find out, so she stammered out a lame response, not used to making excuses. "It's not what you think," she offered, as if she could trick him into not believing his own eyes.

He placed a hand over his heart. "Please, don't worry. I know a few people who are like you."

"What do you mean, like me?"

He stepped closer. The light from the small candle on the table illuminated his face—his firm jaw with a growing stubble of facial hair, the short and neat haircut that highlighted his strong cheek-bones, the gentle glint in his eyes.

"You're a mage, aren't you?" he asked, still whispering, as if afraid to scare her further by raising his voice.

Elice's voice became trapped in her throat.

"I won't tell anyone what I've seen. I promise," he said when she didn't answer.

She forced out a small "thank you," to which he nodded and turned to leave. "Wait!" she shouted, then cringed at herself for being so loud. When he turned, she wondered why she had called him back. "I'm Elice."

"I know who you are," he said, stuffing his hands into his pockets. "Everyone has been talking about Princess Alice's sister. You two look so much alike."

"You know my sister?" She looked him over once more. He was a soldier, as evidenced by his green uniform. Even at this late hour, his attire was in order, as if he just had it washed and pressed.

He nodded his head. "I do. Please, allow me to introduce myself. I'm James." He bent low as he bowed to her, and she gave a curtsey, the toes of her shoes squishing in the mud from all the water she conjured and spilled on the dirt floor.

"You said this was your practice dummy?" She pointed to the sack of fabric that used to look like a mannequin.

He bent down to pick up a few loose strands of yarn. "I usually manage the broken equipment here, so when I saw the state of the last dummy, I wanted to catch the culprit who made such a mess of things." He gave her a pointed stare, but by the way his lips quirked, she knew he was more amused than angry.

"I'm so sorry about the mess," she said, looking around at the state of the shed. Bits of straw and cotton stuck in thick piles to the mud, and shredded pieces of cloth hung on every surface.

He chuckled and tossed the yarn on the ground. "No need to apologize, my princess. I'll make sure it's cleaned up before everyone wakes in the morning."

She felt awful as she pictured him picking up every strand of yarn and hay. "I'll try not to destroy anything else."

"Please, Princess, this shed is yours. I'll keep it well stocked with dummies for you."

After another smile and bow, he excused himself from the room. Elice wondered if she should stop coming to the shed now that someone knew she was using it for magic. She shook her head and thought about finding another spot before she snuck back into the castle.

≈

The clock on the wall of Miss Tabitha's office showed her she was two minutes early. So why was the governess glaring at her as if she had stolen her favorite pair of shoes?

Miss Tabitha spoke through pursed lips. "While I appreciate your attempt, a princess should never arrive early or late, but right on time."

Elice returned her glare. She had gone through the trouble of getting up early enough to make the woman happy, and this was the thanks she got? Another lesson?

Her disposition remained low throughout the morning as she continued reading from the etiquette book while Miss Tabitha was out of the office. She was an hour in when a servant entered the room and bowed.

"Your Highness," he began, "Miss Tabitha would like you to meet her in the ballroom."

"The ballroom?" She squinted, wondering why the woman wanted her to meet there.

The boy only nodded, so Elice shrugged and closed the etiquette book.

She followed him to the ballroom. Inside, a few people with

violins stood beside Miss Tabitha.

"Ah, yes, there you are," Miss Tabitha said and waved her over. There was a man standing next to her, and Elice, with a roll of her eyes, realized he was another potential date for her to meet. "Princess Elice, please meet Lord Brown," she introduced the young man, who bowed. "I was hoping to get you on the dance floor as practice for the celebration."

Elice looked at her with wide eyes. The woman ignored her and waved for the violinists to play. The soft shrill of the violins filled the expansive room and echoed off the walls. As beautiful as it sounded, Elice was mortified.

She side-stepped the man's inviting hand to get closer to Miss Tabitha. "I've never danced before," she whispered.

Tabitha gave her an odd look. "They really didn't have balls at the Great Fort, then?"

Elice didn't answer.

Tabitha leaned in closer. "Just go with it. He's supposed to lead, anyway." She gave Elice a gentle nudge in the young lord's direction.

Elice grabbed his outstretched hands, and the young man snorted. He corrected her grip and pulled her in close.

He let out a groan when she stepped on his foot. "Sorry," she muttered, but he was already looking at her with a raised eyebrow, likely thinking she was the strangest person he'd ever met. He guided her through a box move, and she clumsily followed his steps, keeping her eyes on her own feet the entire time.

After a couple of minutes, Miss Tabitha had enough of watching the train wreck that was Elice's dancing. She thanked Lord

Brown for coming, and Elice watched as he hurried out of the room.

"Wow, that was atrocious," Miss Tabitha said with a grimace.

"I told you." Elice sighed. "Please tell me you don't plan on having me dance anymore today."

Miss Tabitha didn't have to answer, since another young gentleman wearing shiny dance shoes walked into the room. Elice groaned, earning her an admonishing glance from Miss Tabitha.

After several more failed attempts and dirty looks after stepping on many toes, Elice was about ready to give up. She opened her mouth to tell Miss Tabitha she didn't want to continue, but the woman cut in first, speaking to someone behind her.

"Oh, you must be Sir Daniel," Miss Tabitha said. Elice turned to see a soldier in uniform approaching. "I received your request to meet the infamous Princess Elice just this morning. I'm glad to have been able to squeeze you in today."

Elice looked at the man with fresh eyes as he made his way over and bowed his respects. He must be the soldier Andre mentioned last night.

"Thank you for seeing me on such short notice, Your Highness." He bowed again, and Elice gave him an approving nod.

"Thank you for coming," Elice told him. She hoped this would be the last person she would need to meet with, and that she could enjoy his company enough to be her date. This entire process vexed her and made her feel thoroughly uncomfortable, so the sooner she could put an end to it, the better.

It started out well enough. She avoided stepping on his toes, but it meant she focused more on his feet than on his face.

"So," she said, looking up into his dark eyes and then back to his feet again before she missed a step, "you're in the King's Army?"

"I joined the academy at sixteen and was recruited right after graduation. I'm only a sergeant now, but I hope to continue moving up the ranks."

Elice nodded—she could admire the fact that he had aspirations.

"Serving your father," he continued, "has always been a dream of mine. My father was injured in the Last Mage War. I know I'm making him proud by serving the crown."

"So, you enjoy being a soldier?"

"I do. I want to make sure this kingdom remains safe. That's why I admire the king's fierce defense against all those who oppose him—especially mages."

Elice raised an eyebrow and looked up from his feet, almost tripping on the skirt of her dress when she glanced at his face. "What... What did you say?"

"I didn't mean to bring that up. I know how sensitive the subject is, with your relatives being murdered by those evil abominations. Ow!"

She dug her short heel into his shoe and dropped his hands. "Excuse me. I think I'm going to be sick."

As she stomped out of the ballroom, she ignored Miss Tabitha calling out her name, but she couldn't be in that room any longer otherwise she'd do or say something worse than dig her foot into the man's shoe.

∿

Being around so many people was an unfamiliar experience, so it shocked her when it only took a few minutes to cool off the raging heat inside. She drew in several deep breaths, calming her mind and reminding herself that she was not a monster. However, Sir Daniel's words continued to hurt—they dug into her skin and created fresh scars. His words brought back memories of Lenore. The old woman had always told her she would never learn to control her powers.

Elice took another calming breath.

She decided she would prove Lenore wrong—prove them all wrong. Mages weren't evil beings who needed to be feared, and Elice wanted to show she was not some wicked creature that deserved to be locked in a cage—or a cottage.

When she returned to the grand ballroom, Miss Tabitha stood watching the musicians rehearse a new song. She took one look at Elice and stomped her way over, her arms swinging as she stepped with fiery feet.

"I'm sorry," Elice began, but the woman shook her head.

"May I remind you we only have six days until your party? I, for one, would not enjoy watching you dance by yourself in front of three hundred of your most esteemed guests."

"I would honestly prefer that." Elice scowled at herself as soon as she spoke. She had just told herself to behave, and the first thing she did when scolded was back herself further into a corner.

Miss Tabitha narrowed her eyes. "You are nothing like your sister. When I advise her, she always takes heed." She sighed and lowered her hands to her side. "Please, Your Highness, I'm only trying to help you."

"Excuse me," said a voice from behind her. "I hope I'm not too late."

The jolt of shock didn't come from being interrupted—it was from the familiarity of the voice and the consequent blush that rushed to her face.

"Oh," Tabitha exclaimed, shocked as well. "Please, do come in."

Elice turned and stared with wide eyes as the man she met in the shed last night walked toward her.

The governess recovered from her bout with Elice and was back to her normal bravado. "Princess Elice, please meet Captain James Taylor, Lord of Talin."

James's eyes never left Elice's as he reached for her extended hand—it must have moved on its own, because she didn't think she had raised it—and brought the back of it to his lips for a soft kiss. "It's an honor to meet you, Princess."

"Why don't the two of you head to the dance floor?" Miss Tabitha didn't care that Elice shook her head. She gave them both a slight push and then waved to strike up the violinists.

James, still holding her hand, guided her to the middle of the room and spun to face her. The look on her face must have been one of wide-eyed hesitation, because he frowned. "Is something wrong?"

"I..." was all she could stammer out. She looked toward the musicians, now playing their up-tempo arrangement. Elice felt a sinking weight in the pit of her stomach as she thought about stepping on James's toes. Would he laugh at her when he saw she couldn't dance? She wondered if she should have paid more attention to her other dance partners. Why was she so embarrassed all of a sudden?

She swallowed her apprehension and turned to look at him. "I can't dance."

A soft smile touched his lips. "Have you never danced before?"

"Before today? No."

"Well, you'll need a proper teacher." He let her hand go as he turned his attention to the band. He asked them to stop the music, which earned him several bewildered stares. "Can you play it from the top at a slower pace?"

The musicians looked at each other before the lead violinist nodded and began playing.

"The key," James returned his gaze to her, "is to first take it slow. May I?" He motioned for her hands, and she placed them in his.

James slipped her left hand to his shoulder while his free hand came to rest on her waist. When she danced with the other men this morning, she only felt irked at being this close to them. With James holding her this close, her palms became sweaty, and her heart beat loud in her ears.

He began counting out the beats as they stepped in time with the slower tempo. "That's it, just keep counting. Music is about feeling the beat. Try listening with your heart instead of thinking about where your feet are going."

She looked from his feet to his face as they completed their box step. "So, you're a captain?"

He gave a shy smile as he nodded. "I was recently promoted."

She felt silly that she worried about leaving him to clean up the shed last night. Thinking about it with this new information, he would have had one of his subordinates clean up the mess.

She lowered her voice. "The shed was taken care of, then?"

"What shed?" He gave her a smile as he pulled away from her, spun her around once, and then resettled into their original position.

Her breath snagged as a stifled gasp made its way out of her mouth from the surprise twirl. When he chuckled, a laugh escaped her mouth as well. She looked up at him. He was about a foot taller, and she felt drawn in by his dark eyes.

"See," he whispered, a smooth note to his deep voice. "You just needed the right teacher."

She cleared her throat—her mouth became dry as if she hadn't had a drink of water all day. "How did you become a lord at such a young age?"

"My father named me sole heir to his estate, as I'm his only child. He died in the Last Mage War when I was just a year old."

Elice nodded, realizing most people their age lost family in the war. To change the subject, she recalled what she knew of his hometown. "I've read that Talin is a beautiful city."

He grinned—the smile reached all the way to his eyes. "It is, especially in the fall, when the trees change color and the air smells of their leaves."

She could picture the grand beauty of the fall leaves. She used to watch the forest change color around her old cottage, hoping one day to see those leaves up close. Her fingers twitched with the want of releasing a burst of earth magic.

At that moment, the violinists finished their song.

Miss Tabitha almost lost it, running up behind the musicians and waving her hands. "What are you thinking? Keep playing!

She's yet to scare this one off!" They looked at her, appalled, their bows half-lowered as if stuck between two positions.

Elice caught James's amused smile and inwardly groaned. She had never felt this embarrassed before, and she didn't like the way it made her stomach drop.

Miss Tabitha sighed, adjusted her headscarf, and walked to Elice and James as if they didn't hear her outburst. "Lord Talin, you don't have anywhere else to be, do you?" Miss Tabitha didn't wait for his reply. She hooked her arms over their shoulders and all but forced them toward a small table at one end of the great hall. "Come, sit. I'll be back with refreshments." Elice glared at Miss Tabitha's back as she left the room.

"She's never been one for subtlety," James said with a laugh as he settled into his chair.

"I'm sorry about that," Elice said, meeting his eyes from across the table. It relieved her to find that he wore a soft expression.

"Have you been meeting with potential escorts all day?"

She rolled her eyes. "Since yesterday."

"I'm sure you've already met someone you'd like to accompany you to your ball."

"As you heard Miss Tabitha say, I've scared everyone off—not just with my lack of dancing skills."

He leaned forward in his chair. "How is it you've never danced before?"

Elice bit her lip. "I'm sure you've heard that I wasn't raised in the castle."

He looked thoughtful for a moment before answering. "I try not to pay too much attention to gossip, but I have heard talk of it.

Some have said you were raised in Fort Aramu, which is strange because I was there for academy and I'm sure I would have noticed you."

At his comment, she looked away for a moment. How could she have overlooked the fact that Fort Aramu was the location of the King's Academy and where all the new army recruits attended their first training? "I wasn't there. My upbringing is complicated, to put it lightly."

He leaned closer and lowered his voice. "Does it have anything to do with your ... abilities?"

"Yes," she whispered. "My parents ... were afraid. When I was born, they sent me off to live with someone who was supposed to help me learn to control my powers. But I never did. Instead, I think I've just gotten stronger."

He blinked at her and gave a slight shake of his head. "They just sent you off? Who did you live with?"

Elice chewed on the inside of her lip again. She looked around the room, worried about sharing too much. "With a woman named Lenore."

"Madam Lenore?" His eyes grew wide. "Why her? I can't believe they would trust her."

Elice nodded, wondering why everyone seemed to know about her old guardian. After reading from her mother's book, though, she could see why society viewed Lenore as untrustworthy. "Apparently it had something to do with a vision she had. But ... we believe she lied about it. And now I'm stuck in the palace when I should be off finding her."

He grew quiet for a long moment, studying her face with an

unreadable expression. "You're the reason for the lockdown." It wasn't a question, so he didn't wait for an answer. "You're not allowed to leave."

"I'm not, and that means I'll never know the truth." She looked down at her lap.

"Well," he said as he sat straight in his chair and eyed the door. "If you're looking for a way to escape, you would be happy to know that the guard by the east tower gate usually falls asleep on duty around midnight."

Her eyes lit up at his suggestion. "You're sure?"

"It's awful, really, but it happens without fail."

Elice sat back in her seat as she stared at the man before her. "I'm so glad I met you."

The grin on his face took her breath away. "When I first received the invitation from Miss Tabitha, I didn't plan on coming. Then I met you last night and knew the Fates must have wanted me to meet you."

She raised an eyebrow in question.

He laughed and scratched at the back of his head. "Long story short: I never come to these kinds of things."

She thanked the Fates he came this time.

Eleven

Elice didn't know if she could get used to Miss Tabitha's glare, but there she stood, once again caught in the woman's fierce glower.

"What did you do?" the woman almost growled at her. "I thought you two were getting along! Please tell me you didn't ruin it." There were four servants behind her, carrying large trays full of plates of food and pitchers of drink.

Elice shrugged her shoulders. "He said he had a meeting to attend."

Tabitha waved the servants away and then turned to Elice with a raised eyebrow. "So, you didn't frighten him off?"

"Don't get too excited, Miss Tabitha." Elice rolled her eyes as the woman sat with her at the table.

"Princess, you aren't excited enough. You don't understand who you just met."

"You mean James? Why would I get excited?" She tried to be relaxed about it, but the waves in her stomach continued to roll around these last few minutes after talking with him.

Tabitha scoffed at her. "Well, I may be a few years older than you, but even I can appreciate how handsome Lord Talin is. He is the most eligible bachelor in all of Norraine, yet he has no interest in balls or gossip of any kind. Naturally, all the girls your age fawn over him. I've never heard of him showing anyone special attention, but he seemed to be taken by you."

Elice's cheeks burned at Tabitha's words. "I'm sure he was just being nice."

Tabitha shook her head. "Either way, there are no other bachelors who can appear with you on such short notice. You must decide today who you want as your date."

At her words, Elice felt as if someone had lit a fire underneath her chair. "I'm not ready to decide yet."

She still had to find out if James's tip was true and if she could leave the castle to go in search of Lenore. She finally had an opportunity, and she couldn't miss it. If this was her chance to get out, she was going to take it. Then she wouldn't have to worry about a silly ball.

"You're running out of time, Princess. If you don't choose someone soon, you will end up going alone."

"I've been alone before, Miss Tabitha. It's not so bad." Even though she said it, the words rang hollow in her head. She always wanted to be amongst the world, and now she couldn't imagine ever being alone again—not like before, in that lonely cottage.

Tabitha stared at her with pursed lips. "You didn't grow up at

Fort Aramu, did you?"

Elice took a deep breath before shaking her head. "No, I didn't."

"It's not my place to question you or the royal family. You must have your reasons for lying."

Elice debated telling the woman the truth. Tabitha seemed to love gossip—or at least to be on the receiving end of gossip, which was just as bad. However, Elice wanted to trust the woman. Her heart desperately wanted to find a friend she could talk to about her family. "I didn't live with family, either, and until this week, I didn't know who my actual parents were."

Tabitha's face grew serious as she hummed. "Now I see why you're so troubled."

"I guess I am troubled," Elice admitted. "I'm not over what happened, and I don't even know why it happened."

"It seems to me you need closure so you can move on and start living your life."

"It would help if I had more time before deciding on a date." Elice gave her an alluring smile, to which Miss Tabitha rolled her eyes.

"You can have until the end of the day. Come see me at my office before dinnertime."

She half-heartedly agreed before she left the ballroom. Elice had many things to think about, and she needed advice. Unfortunately, the only person she could go to was her sister. Knowing as much as she knew about her twin so far, she knew what Alice would tell her.

She found Alice hiding away in her study—a paintbrush in her hand and a pensive look on her face. Elice knocked on the open doorway, causing her sister to look up from scrutinizing one of her paintings.

"Elice, please, come in," Alice said, distracted, although the smile she gave let Elice know she wasn't mad at the disruption.

"I haven't seen you all day," Elice remarked as she pulled up a stool. She watched as Alice dipped the end of her brush into the blob of red paint on her color palette and then colored in a flower petal on the canvas in front of her. Her eyebrows quirked as she realized Alice was drawing the same flower again.

"I've been in council meetings with Father." Alice sighed. Elice wasn't sure if the sigh was in response to the meetings or the painting, since Alice dipped her brush into the blue paint to mix with the red before adding it to the flower. It looked like she was experimenting with another shade of red—this time, it looked darker.

"I've been dancing all day."

Alice turned, her paintbrush held between her teeth as she poured the last of the red paint onto her palette. She removed the brush before she spoke. "Miss Tabitha tried that bit on you, then? I bet it was awkward."

"It was at first, but then I ended up meeting someone who ...wasn't terrible."

Alice gave Elice her full attention. "Really?"

Elice squirmed on her stool. "That's what I wanted to talk to you about, actually. I first met him last night when I snuck into the barracks."

The paintbrush dropped to the ground, smearing dark red paint on the tiled floor. "Elice!"

"Well, it was technically my second time sneaking out." She went on to explain how she needed to release her pent-up magical energy, found the abandoned shed where she met the soldier, and how he showed up to meet with her in the ballroom.

Alice shook her head. "I can't believe you snuck out in the middle of the night. Who was this mysterious soldier?"

"His name is James."

"James Taylor?" Alice's jaw dropped open. "I can't believe he actually showed up."

"That's exactly what Miss Tabitha said."

"He's avoided parties for months now. Even when he was younger, he loathed them."

"He made it seem as if you knew each other."

Alice's face fell as she looked down at her hands. "We do. Actually, it was always the three of us—James, Andre, and me. We were inseparable whenever their families came to the castle. Their mothers were widows, so our mother spent lots of time with them after the war."

"What happened?" Elice folded her hands on her lap as she listened.

"I don't know. One day, Andre and James stopped talking to each other. I think they had a falling out."

Elice furrowed her eyebrows at her sister. "You never asked them?"

Alice shrugged. "I figured they would tell me if they wanted me to know. I was sad at first. James was a good friend. Suddenly, he stopped coming around, and then he was off to join the academy."

"Were you two..."

"You mean, were we a couple?" Alice shook her head with an amused smile on her lips.

This was the perfect moment for the question she had wanted to ask. "What about you and Andre? Are you in love with him?"

This time Alice laughed. "By the Fates, no, I'm not in love with him. He's my best friend—I love him like a brother. He's been there for me when no one else was, but I've never thought of him as anything more. He feels the same way, too."

Elice didn't understand it at all. "Then why are you still engaged to him? Don't you want to marry someone you love?"

"Elice," she said with a serious note. "I know you don't see it the same way I do because you grew up the way you did. I agreed to marry Dre because that's how I was raised. If I am to be queen, then I need to put the kingdom before myself."

"What does that have to do with marrying someone you don't love?"

"I could never marry who I want. The Fates haven't written it that way for me." There was a tone to her words that made her voice ring with sorrow.

Elice looked at her sister with a raised eyebrow. "Is there someone you do want to marry instead of Andre?"

Alice's face blushed as she turned toward her canvas. "It wouldn't matter if there was."

"By the Fates, Alice. There is someone!"

"Shh!" Alice put a finger to her mouth as she looked at Elice in horror.

"Who is it? Please tell me it's not Lord Mead with his greedy smirk."

Alice looked around as if there were others in the room with them. "There is someone." When Elice shrieked, Alice shushed her again. "You can't tell anyone!"

"Who would I tell?" Elice asked. "Besides, you're keeping my magic a secret from the entire kingdom. I would never tell anyone about your secret."

Alice smiled at her and reached for her hands. "I know you wouldn't. I've just never told anyone. Well, Andre knows, but he figured it out on his own."

"He knows you love someone else?" Elice gave her a disbelieving stare.

"Of course. He's my best friend, remember? He knew before I even realized how I felt."

"I really don't understand any of this."

Alice sighed and put her palette on the floor. "He's a commoner, Elice. I could never marry him because he doesn't have a title and is not from a noble family. He owns an art shop in town—that's where we met."

"So he's an artist like you?"

Alice's cheeks turned red, and she nodded. "His name's Donovan."

"I wish I could meet him." Elice put a comforting hand on her sister's shoulder.

"He'll be at our birthday ball—working, of course. Father hired him to paint scenes of the ball."

"Then I can't wait to meet him."

"Please don't make it awkward for me."

Elice made a face. "Am I really that bad?"

This time, Alice gave her a comforting pat. "You're just learning."

She felt patronized, but Alice either ignored her expression or didn't notice as she stood and cleaned up her supplies. "Anyway, I think you'll be too distracted by your date."

"I haven't even chosen anyone yet." Elice didn't mention she planned an escape that very night.

"Your only option is James, and you know it. He's handsome, rich, and the youngest person in history to make the rank of captain."

"By the Fates, Alice, you sound so shallow."

Alice laughed at her. "You can't tell me you don't think he's cute."

Elice responded by pursing her lips into a tight line.

∼

The sun hung low in the sky by the time Elice spotted him. She stood from the bench she read at and hurried to catch up to him.

"Lord Copita," she said, just loud enough to get his attention. Andre was walking with two other soldiers, and they all turned at the call.

"Princess Elice!" Andre's face split into a grin. He waved at his two companions, then made his way toward her. "What brings you out here?"

They were just inside the military encampment, where the central buildings opened up to an outdoor gathering area. Several soldiers of the King's Army grouped together around a large fire pit, unwinding after a long day. There were many young men and a few women, some still in uniform, but most dressed in trousers and a simple shirt. Elice had even seen a couple of men without shirts, enjoying the beginning of summer weather.

"I was looking for you, actually," Elice answered when they reached each other at the halfway point.

"To what do I owe the pleasure?" He stood with his hands on his hips, the top buttons of his shirt undone. She forced her eyes to stay on his, though he had a coy look in them that made Elice blush.

"I was hoping we could talk somewhere more private."

She couldn't read the look he gave her. A few passersby turned with questioning glances in their direction, which made Elice wonder if she had used the wrong choice of words. All the social skills she had learned growing up did not prepare her for the real world, and not even Miss Tabitha's lessons had been enough to help her just yet.

"Of course," he said, his voice eager. "Let's go to my office." He gestured toward the building on her right.

"No," Elice blurted, thinking his office would be an inappropriate choice. "It's a beautiful night. Let's stay outside."

He smirked at her, but nodded his head. "We could stargaze. I know the perfect spot."

"What I have to ask won't take that long."

"Oh." He cocked his head to the side. "You wanted to ask me something?"

Elice nodded and walked away from the main entryway, Andre following close behind. She came to a stop near the back of the building, away from prying ears, but still close enough to the stone pathway to avoid suspicion. At least she knew how improper it would be if someone caught the two of them together, hiding behind a building for a secret chat.

"If this is about Daniel—" he began, but Elice interrupted him.

"You mean the bigot who hates mages?" She narrowed her eyes at him when he laughed.

"I didn't know about that! Did he say something? I can make him join the night guard for a few days."

"It's really not that important," she said, but she placed her hands on her hips, and her eyes became thin slits.

"Are you sure about that? You look upset." He took a step toward her, and she could see a smear of dirt on his neck. She was staring at it longer than she should have and snapped her eyes up. He had a knowing smile on his lips when their eyes met.

To change the subject, she brought up the reason she came to talk to him. "What can you tell me about James Taylor?" Right away, she saw the way the name hit him across his face like a blast of hot air.

"How do you know him?"

"Miss Tabitha invited him to meet with me." She omitted the fact that they had met on their own the night before. Not everyone needed to know that, she reasoned.

"You mean he actually showed up?" He huffed in disbelief. Then he fixed his face with a casual aloofness. "How did it go?"

"It went fine, actually."

He shook his head. "That's because you don't know him like I do."

She raised an eyebrow at him and crossed her arms. "He seemed all right to me. I'm thinking of asking him to be my date."

"You're not serious."

"What if I am?" She gave him time to answer, but he only stared at her, unwilling to answer. "What happened between you two? Alice said you had a falling out."

"All you need to know is that he's a jerk." He took another step closer and reached for her folded arms. "You trust me, don't you?"

She swallowed the lump in her throat. "You found me in that abandoned cottage and brought me to my real family because somehow you knew I didn't belong there. I don't know how to repay you for that."

He raised a hand toward her face, but she grabbed his wrist before he could touch her. His smile wavered for a fraction of a second.

"But it doesn't mean I'll take your word on everything you say. So, tell me why I shouldn't trust James."

He lowered his hand and chuckled at her. "You really are one of a kind, Elice."

"And you're stalling—or do you not have anything bad to say about him?"

He sighed. "I must insist that it's something strictly between him and I."

"He doesn't have any idea what you're mad about."

"Is that what he told you?" He raised an inquisitive eyebrow.

"I don't have time for this, Andre." Unsatisfied with the conversation, she turned to walk away, but he caught her by the arm.

"I only tell you this because I care for you."

Her expression softened at his words. "I know, but that doesn't help me with my birthday party situation at all."

He laughed but shook his head. "I suppose not. You'll just have to take my word for it—or don't, that's up to you. Apparently, you won't take anyone's advice."

"Been talking to Miss Tabitha?"

"That's what everyone who comes in contact with you says." She smacked his shoulder, even though she wanted to knock him on his back again with a powerful blast of magic as he continued to laugh at her.

She walked away with burning cheeks and wondered how Alice could ever put up with him. Yet a smile stayed plastered to her face, even though she told herself to wipe it off.

~

It was five minutes to midnight as she made her way to the east tower gate. Elice donned a dark blue hooded cloak in case James was mistaken, and she ended up getting caught. She walked with stealth, avoiding the main halls of the castle as she walked to the back door that led to the outer fields.

When she closed to castle doors behind her—she thanked the Fates she didn't run into anyone in the halls—she adjusted the hood slightly so she could study her surroundings. There was no one outside—no movement, no sound, not even the wind threatened to rebel against her. She took creeping steps toward the outer wall and the guard station in front of the gate, careful not to step on a twig or leaf that might crunch beneath her feet.

Peering into the small booth, she heard the telltale sound of sleep. A large man with a thick gray beard sat on a stool, halfway leaning off it and against the stone wall. His bulky chest moved in time with his snores. He looked too old for this job—his gray hair and the wrinkles on his tanned skin told Elice he was at least fifty years old. She didn't know why he was still in service, but she thanked the Fates again as she turned away from the station and faced the gate.

She eased it open with a grunt, the heavy metal letting out a tiny screech. Biting her lip, she squinted and waited for the guard to yell at her to stop. As the seconds passed and no such yell came, she hurried out of the gate and pushed it shut.

She was outside the castle walls for the first time in days, free to do what she needed to find the truth.

Elice took one step and ran right into the waiting arms of another hooded figure. She let out a gasp in shock and readied her magic for a fight.

"It's me," the person under the hood said before he pulled it back to reveal his face.

"James!" Elice yelped in a harsh whisper. "What are you doing here?"

"I wanted to see for myself if you really were crazy enough to leave," he whispered back. "You're going out there by yourself?"

Elice lowered her hood. "Of course. I told you why I need to do this."

He nodded his head. "I know you have your reasons. Perhaps you think it's better to do it this way—to sneak out in the middle of the night. But if I know King Edgar as well as I think I do, it will only anger him. He would send his troops after you."

"I don't care how angry he'd get. I'm angry as well. He can send his whole army for all I care." She pulled the hood over her head again.

"You deserve to be angry. I get it. But there has to be a better way." He continued to stand in front of her, blocking her path of escape.

Elice crossed her arms over her chest. "You were the one who told me about the sleeping guard. You gave me the idea to escape this way."

James sighed. "I know, and I'm sorry. I don't know what I was thinking."

"You do know why. You just said you didn't think I would actually do it." She was furious that everyone seemed to doubt her.

"I shouldn't have said it that way." He moved out of her way to allow her to pass, but she stayed where she was, waiting for him to continue. "We can't keep talking here. It's bound to draw attention. Besides, there's something I think you'll like to see first." He gestured away from the gate toward a door on the side of the tower.

She hesitated a moment before nodding her head in agreement. It would be better to leave this area before the guard woke up or someone else stumbled upon them.

He led her past the wooden door, holding her hand to help her since only a single dim lantern lit the space. "This tower doesn't have a guard station on top. We'll have to be quiet, though, and stay out of sight in case the guards in the neighboring tower spot us."

Elice could only see the first few steps of the wooden staircase as they began their ascent, still holding onto each other's hands. The staircase spiraled as they climbed, with only the stars in the sky above them and the lanterns spaced every few feet above them lighting their way. When they reached the top, he guided her toward the western-facing edge, and she stared in wonder at the view before her.

She could see the entire castle and the tip of the sprawling city outside the defensive wall. The gray stones of the palace shined yellow, illuminated by a few lanterns strategically attached along the outer walls. The four towering columns of the castle reached into the dark sky—its long stems seemed never-ending as they disappeared into the darkness. In the background, she could make out some of the shops she had passed on her first day in the city. The beauty mesmerized her and stole her breath.

"I understand why you want to leave," James said, stirring Elice out of her enchantment. "As beautiful as this place is, it's not home. You didn't grow up here, you don't know anyone, and the only person you ever knew is out there somewhere." He pointed out past the city.

Elice bounced her head in agreement. "So, why show me this gorgeous view?"

"Because from the moment I met you, I knew you didn't like to play by the rules. That was clear by the way you snuck around the castle and destroyed my things with magic." They both laughed before he continued. "But what you want to do, what you want to accomplish, will take more than just rule breaking."

"What is it you think I want?" she asked him. She didn't know what her answer would be, beyond finding Lenore, so she was curious to hear what he thought she might want.

He turned toward the picturesque backdrop with a contemplative look. "Truth, honesty, a life worth living. You want to find your place in the world—to feel happiness and love." He looked at her again with the most serious expression she'd ever seen.

"How did you know that?" Her voice was breathless, taken away by the reality he had just given her.

"Because I want that too. Everyone wants that. But in order to get it, we must choose the right path."

Elice looked out over the ledge. "How do we even know what the right path is?"

"Honestly, I think only you can answer that question."

She turned, facing the edge of the Jani Forest off in the distance to the east, and leaned against the waist-high wall, her hands gripping the ledge behind her. "Maybe I shouldn't leave tonight. I don't know how to find Lenore anyway, and I don't have any supplies. I'll get lost and dehydrated before I even find her. But I still have to do something."

James mimicked her stance along the wall. "Have you tried diplomacy?"

She raised an eyebrow at him. "I think I ruined any hope of that with the king. He'll see me coming no matter what angle I use on him, since he already knows I want to leave."

He shrugged his shoulders. "Your father is a smart man, but he's not impractical. If you can show him the importance of your mission, he might surprise you."

"Mission?" Elice smiled at the thought, the feeling of purpose swirling around the word. "I like the sound of that."

They shared another quiet laugh before they let the sound fade into the night. Elice looked sideways at him to find that he was staring at her.

"Why does Andre not trust you?" she asked him.

James's smile fell from his face. "To this day, I don't know."

"Alice told me you three used to be friends."

He nodded his head. "Best friends."

"Andre seems to think you should know," she tried again.

"I don't know what I did or what I said. I've tried asking him, but he refuses to tell me. He just assumes I'm unwilling to own up it, whatever *it* is."

Elice pursed her lips for a moment, thinking over his and Andre's words. "He warned me not to trust you."

James pushed off the wall and stood in front of her. "You don't strike me as a person who blindly follows someone else. But if you don't trust me yet, I understand."

She eased herself off the wall as well and stood almost toe-to-toe with him. "I didn't say that. I honestly don't know either of you well enough to believe anything you both say."

"Then I will earn your trust, my princess."

"Please, call me Elice."

"I could never do that."

She rolled her eyes at him, but he only smiled in return. "Can I ask you another question?"

"Anything."

"Will you accompany me to my birthday ball?"

A genuine smile lit up his face, shining in the darkness. "It would be my pleasure."

Twelve

"Alice, wake up." Elice nudged her sister's shoulder.

Alice blinked at her and spoke with a mumble. "What time is it?"

"Almost two, I think," Elice answered before she slid under the blankets, lying on her side with her hand propping her head up.

"In the middle of the night?" Alice seemed more awake now as she supported her head as well.

"I want to tell you what just happened."

"Please tell me you didn't sneak out to practice magic again." A worried note rang in her voice.

"I didn't," Elice answered, and even in the dark room, she could see Alice's skepticism. "I actually snuck out to leave the castle."

"By the Fates!" Alice shrieked. "Father would be furious."

"Please, don't tell him."

"Of course I won't. I'll have a hard time not telling Mother, though, since she's constantly asking me how you are and what you're up to."

"Why is she asking you and not me?" Elice asked. She knew how infrequent her conversations with the queen were. Now she realized that, aside from dinnertime talks, she never really spoke to her mother.

Alice gave her a look. "She's afraid you'll yell at her like you yell at Father."

Elice was going to say she wouldn't yell, but she knew it would have been a lie. "I take it she doesn't do well with confrontation."

"I take after her in that regard. While you most certainly take after Father. He almost chases after conflict, even as he grows older."

Elice saw herself running into conflict often, even when living with Lenore.

"If you left the castle," Alice continued hesitantly, "why did you come back?"

Elice recounted her run-in with Lord Talin and their talk at the top of the tower. By the end, her cheeks had flushed with heat, and she was glad for the darkness so Alice wouldn't see it.

"James was always the most mature out of the three of us," Alice told her and then yawned. "I'm glad you didn't listen to Andre. You and James would make a good match. You should marry someone you get along with."

Alice rolled over, pulling the blankets over her shoulders.

"Alice, what did you say?" When Alice didn't answer, Elice nudged her back and spoke with more force. "Did you say something about marriage?" She leaned over her sister's body and saw she was fast asleep.

With a groan, she rolled out of the bed and crept back to her bedchamber. At this rate, she would only get a few hours of restless sleep before she met Miss Tabitha.

In the morning, she showed up at Miss Tabitha's office right on time. She knew it upset the woman that she skipped out on meeting her last night, so she intended to be on her best behavior for once.

Before she could receive a scolding—Miss Tabitha already had one of her hips cocked to the side, a fisted hand resting on it—she blurted out an apology befitting a princess. "Thank you for waiting for me to give you news about my date. You'll be happy to know I've chosen someone, and I've already asked him."

Miss Tabitha eyed her. "Well, I'll forgive you for not telling me last night since you showed up on time today, *and* because you decided." She then returned to her normal exuberant demeanor and clapped her hands with excitement. "So, who did you pick?"

Elice clasped her hands behind her back. "I chose Captain Taylor."

The woman shrieked, and Elice's face wrinkled at the sound. "*And...* What did he say?"

"He said yes," she answered, earning another squeal from Tabitha.

"I have so much to do! I'll have to update the programs and order a coordinating outfit for Lord Talin. Oh! He'll need to be measured by the seamstress! By the Fates, there are only five days left!"

Miss Tabitha rushed out of the room, leaving Elice alone in the office. She huffed a laugh before grabbing the dreadful etiquette book from the desk. When Miss Tabitha returned an hour later, she was still in a frenzy, rattling off about the many last-minute things that needed adjusting or completing.

"I know you keep saying it's such an important day," Elice said when the woman took a break to sit at her desk. "But I still don't see why everyone is making such a big fuss about it. It's just a birthday. I'll have another one next year."

"Oh, Princess Elice," Miss Tabitha responded with a heavy exhalation. "I know you're not accustomed to such clamor. In the public arena that is part of palace life, the citizens must see you with a proper gentleman. I'm sure you're already aware how fast gossip can spread."

She nodded. "Is that why Alice became engaged so young? She mentioned something about marriage last night."

Miss Tabitha rummaged through a stack of papers on her desk. "The king had that planned for a long time."

"Well, I'm glad I don't have to worry about it. I'm definitely not ready to even talk about marriage."

The woman hummed from behind a sheet of paper.

"A forced dated to the ball is enough for me."

Miss Tabitha knocked the stack of papers, scattering them across the floor.

Elice stood from her seat to help pick up the mess. "It *is* just a date, right?"

"Oh, I'm not good with secrets!" She threw the papers back to the ground with a huff.

"What secrets are you keeping from me?" She eyed the woman

before her.

Miss Tabitha groaned. "Your parents didn't want you to know this right away. They were planning on easing you into it. I thought it wasn't right, especially now that I know about your tumultuous relationship with them. But who am I to go against the King and Queen?"

"Miss Tabitha..." Elice said, wary to continue. "What are they keeping from me?"

"It's not uncommon," she muttered, "for the escort to be ... an actual suitor ... or an intended betrothed."

Elice coughed, choking on the words as if Miss Tabitha had forced them down her throat. "Betrothed? Like engaged? To be wed?"

"Yes, Your Highness, that's what a betrothal is."

Elice shook her head. "I know what it means. But does it mean, by me asking James to be my date, I really asked him to..."

Miss Tabitha stood and walked to the desk with the papers in hand. "It will all work out by the Fates' design. Besides, you can't do much better than Captain Taylor."

"That's not the point," Elice objected. She followed Tabitha to the desk. "It's like they're trying to get rid of me again. And the last thing I'm thinking about is marriage."

The governess placed a reassuring hand on the girl's arm, though no amount of comfort would help her through this. She would need a way out—this time, without breaking any rules.

⌒

Elice controlled herself until dinner. It was the usual company—her parents, her sister, and Andre—and the usual flow of conversation. The men shared a discourse of the military's condition as of today, while Alice and Julice talked about all they accomplished. Elice sat in her seat and avoided inserting herself into their discussions, eating her meal in small bites.

"Elice," the queen called out during dessert. She snapped her eyes in her mother's direction. "I spoke with Miss Tabitha today. She informed me you now have a date for the party."

"Right," she said after she swallowed a bite of cake. All eyes focused on her, which made her swallow again. "I've asked Lord Talin."

"Captain Taylor?" the king interjected. When Elice nodded, he spoke with veneration. "He's one of my high-ranking officers and the youngest member of the council."

"It's a fine choice, Elice," her mother said, smiling.

Elice dug her fork into her slice but didn't bring it to her mouth. She looked across the table. Alice looked at her with interest, while Andre avoided eye contact. Elice didn't know what to make of his expression, or the lack thereof.

Since she had her parent's attention, she decided to take James's advice. She placed her fork down and cleared her throat. "I'm glad you brought it up. Why did you feel the need to hide the fact that I'm now engaged?"

Her mother's eyes widened, and her father sputtered over the rim of his wineglass.

"We didn't want to overwhelm you," he said after he wiped his mouth with his napkin.

It was true, then—she was engaged. Elice wanted to scream at them. An angry tirade of words threatened to escape her mouth like a fiery flame. Instead, she inhaled and pushed out her anger with an exhalation. "So, you want to marry me off to get rid of me?" It was difficult to keep the underlying heat out of her words.

"That's not it, Elice," her mother beseeched her. "You must understand how we do things."

Elice shook her head. "That's the problem, though. I don't understand. I don't want to think about marriage—I don't want to even think about a birthday party."

"Elice," her father said in warning.

She had prepared, however, to work this out in her favor. James's words echoed in her mind all day, and she had rehearsed what to say to get her father to do what she wanted—by making him think it would benefit *him*.

"So, I have a bargain for you," she began, remembering Lenore's negotiations with him all those years ago.

King Edgar placed his elbows on the table—a major etiquette mistake, Elice noted with a smile—and steepled his fingers. "A bargain? You wish to barter?"

Elice nodded and took a deep breath. "In exchange for my good behavior, you will summon Lenore to the castle."

He stared at her with a calculating look, though he didn't put up a fight right away. For good measure, she added, "And I want to postpone any talk of marriage until after Alice's wedding. In order for me to start my new life, I need closure. The least you can do is help me close the door on my past." She thanked the Fates Miss Tabitha gave her those words to use.

"To be clear," he responded after several moments, "you want me to summon Lenore and postpone your engagement in exchange for your good behavior—no more fussing or stomping on others' toes?"

"Yes," she answered with a cringe, remembering her awful dancing, then added, "and if she doesn't show up the day after the party, you will send your best man to search for her and bring her here."

Edgar hummed. "I believe we can make this work. You have a deal, Elice."

Elice smiled, feeling rather proud of herself. She was on her way to accomplishing her mission, and all it cost her was a few days of her best behavior. What did she have to lose?

As she scanned the table, she saw everyone's mouth gaped in shock. She wondered how long it had been since the king was last outsmarted. She knew the answer—Lenore was likely the last person to outwit him. Shrugging, she returned to her cake with a smile.

∼

With her father's biography in her hands, she inhaled a sharp breath for courage and knocked on the door. A soft voice responded, telling her to come in. After another deep breath, she pushed open her mother's office door.

The queen looked up from her book and set her pen down. "Elice," she said, her voice high pitched from the shock of seeing her daughter enter the room. "Please, come in."

Elice hesitated a moment before walking closer to her mother's desk. "Is it a bad time?"

Julice gave a gentle smile and waved her closer. "Not at all. I just finished up for the day."

Elice nodded, though she continued to stand in the middle of the room, unsure if she was prepared to have this conversation with her mother.

Julice, noticing her apprehension, pointed to the chair across from her desk. "Would you like to sit?"

Without responding, Elice walked to the desk and placed the tome on top of it. "I need to ask you about something."

Julice met her eyes. "What do you want to talk about, my dear?"

"The day Lenore turned on Orser. Surely you didn't really trust her, did you?"

Julice opened the book to a random page. "I wrote all about our encounter with Madam Lenore and how we didn't fully trust her."

Elice wanted to huff an impatient sigh. "I know. I read through it. But honestly, how could you trust her even a little? Sure, she led Father to the Blood Flower. He destroyed it, and that's how he was able to defeat Orser. But after everything she had done, it just doesn't seem fair she got to live out the rest of her days in freedom."

Julice shut the book and pushed it away, unable to look at it anymore. "What do you know of the Fire Lords?"

"Just the basics—they were the fire mages who rebelled against the kingdom. There's not much about them in your book, or any other book in the library, for that matter." She knew Orser was the leader of the Fire Lords, and in their attempted overthrow of the kingdom, Orser killed her great-grandfather with his fire magic. That was thirty years ago. Her grandfather became king, but after only a ten-year reign, he was also struck down by Orser, paving the way for her father to become king at just seventeen.

Julice nodded and pursed her lips. "Most of their information is secret to the world."

Elice shook her head. "That's not what I want to talk about, though. What I want to know is why you trusted Lenore in the first place?"

Julice sat for a long moment without answering. Elice thought her mother wouldn't answer until she sighed and met her eyes again. "I didn't trust her, and neither did your father. We did what we had to do—"

"For the good of the kingdom," Elice interrupted with a frown, "I know." She blew out an impatient breath and looked at the desk. Her eyes caught sight of a familiar book and it made her heart clench. "Were you writing in the family tree?"

With a shy smile, Julice turned the book around to face Elice. "I should've written this page correctly the first time. When Alice told me you found it, I knew it had upset you because your name wasn't inscribed on a branch. So, I finally fixed it."

Elice eyed the book before she pulled it closer. Underneath her parents' names and next to Alice's, she saw a beautiful branch with her name written on it. Tears welled up in her eyes at the sight of the curvy script. When she looked up, her mother shared a similar look as a tear rolled down her cheek.

As if on cue, they both stood and ran to the other side of the desk, collapsing in each other's arms.

∽

Later that night, instead of staying in her room like she ought to, Elice wandered back to the storage shed. If she was being honest with herself, she knew she wanted to run into James again and tell him what happened with her father—though the chance to use her magic was always a welcome opportunity.

After only a few minutes of practice, she heard the door creak open. Of course, her ears were straining for the sound in anticipation of his arrival.

His smile was like another candle in the dark room. "And here I thought you'd make another run for it," he said after he closed the door behind him.

Elice, already covered in strands of hay, wiped the front of her green dress to straighten out her appearance. "Well, you readied this dummy for me. I couldn't let your effort go to waste. Besides, I wanted to thank you for your advice. I worked out a deal with my father."

James grinned as he stepped closer to her in the small room. "You negotiated with him? How did it go?"

"I got him to agree to summon Lenore."

"What do you have to do in exchange?" He quirked an eyebrow.

"I have to be good," she answered with an eye roll.

James laughed and pointed at the obliterated dummy. "Does this count as being good?"

Elice turned away from him to hide her blush. "I need to expel my magical energy somehow. I'd rather do it in the dead of night than in the middle of the day, when it's easier for someone to walk in on me."

"Is your magic so powerful that you need to discharge it?" he asked.

Elice nodded. "I don't know what it's like for other mages, but if I don't release my magic, it will come out on its own. Lenore and I tested this out when I was younger. I can only go a few days before I explode—the energy will just force its way out."

"I don't think that's normal. Otherwise, we would have heard of other mages going through the same thing."

"Lenore always told me I wasn't a normal mage. She said I would cause destruction if I let my powers go unchecked, which is why I practiced keeping it contained. It never helped, though. When she wasn't around, I could let myself go. That's when I feel better—when I use my powers to their fullest extent."

"What did she mean? Did she have visions of something bad happening if you use your powers that way?"

Elice shook her head. "She never shared her visions with me. All I know is how I feel. If I don't use it, I feel horrible. I can't think straight, and my body shakes with the need to release it. But when I use it... I don't know how to describe it."

"Can you show me?" he asked. His eyes gleamed with interest and curiosity.

She smirked and held her hand out, willing the surrounding air and water molecules to gather in her hand to create the spinning storm. Over the last few days, she had gotten better at sustaining control over the small waterspouts she created on her palm. Before, the storm was a mere four inches; now, she held a swirling mass over a foot tall and four inches wide.

The storm picked up more air, water, and speed, threatening to tear through her flesh. She felt the gusts topple over as if it wanted to make a run for it in this small shed. She remained calm, however; speaking to it in her mind as if she knew its very soul. It stayed where it was, coddled in her hand and waving its tendrils of wind at James as if greeting him.

James stared with his mouth ajar. He took a tentative step closer. "That's incredible. Can I touch it?"

Elice shook her head. "I don't want you to get hurt."

"I don't think you'd hurt me," he said, meeting her eyes before he reached his hand forward.

Elice pulled back in shock as the tornado smacked his hand away. James gasped at first, then let out a burst of laughter. Elice couldn't help the shaky breath of a laugh that escaped her mouth.

With a grin, he reached his hand toward the storm once more, this time much slower. Elice spoke to the storm, asking it to slow just enough for him to put his hand through it. It was fascinating—the slow speed at which it swirled made it seem as if it moved in slow motion. James waved his hand back and forth inside of it, an amused smile on his face as he played with the slow-moving spirals. She had fun as well, willing it to bend and twist over his hand in a soft caress.

"Your magic is beautiful," he said, looking into her eyes.

She had never heard those words uttered about her magic before. The feeling in her heart echoed through the wind as it hummed in agreement. It swelled with a pride and esteem that she had never felt before. All along, she wondered how important her magic was—at least, she knew it was important to her. She wished to share this experience with the entire world, if only they wouldn't fear her.

She opened her mouth to thank him, but didn't get the chance.

The shed's door opened, and she dropped her spell. Water splashed to the ground, and the surrounding air came to a sudden stop as an elderly man popped his head in.

Her heart pounded in her head as all the blood rushed to it. James lowered his hand, and she realized with embarrassment that hers still hovered in midair, yet she couldn't find the command of it at the moment.

The man, wearing a tan servant's uniform, held a broom in one hand and a lantern in the other. He looked between them before his eyes dawned with realization. He clicked his tongue and then snickered. "There's always a bad egg in every royal family."

Thirteen

King Edgar sat on his elegant, high-backed throne. He wore a red robe over his nightclothes, his face set like stone, and his thick hair pressed down on one side as if he didn't have time to comb it before he appeared in the throne room.

Elice and James stood before him, having been ushered inside by Thomas, the caretaker. When he found them in the shed several minutes earlier, he had threatened to wake the king, but they followed him inside the palace willingly. As her father took steadying breaths and balled his hands into tight fists, Elice wondered if she should have at least put up a fight.

"I can't express," he began, then took another deep breath, "how disappointed I am." He set his gaze upon James with fury. "I thought I could trust you with my daughter because you are a hard worker and your father was one of my greatest friends. I didn't expect to find you sneaking around with her in an empty shed in the middle of the night, doing Fates knows what."

Elice cut her father off before he said something he couldn't take back. "It's not what you think. I was practicing magic, and James was just passing by." She was only a few days off from the truth, she reasoned. It would only hurt the situation more to say it was now their third late-night meeting at that shed, and she was not stupid enough to bring up the time she snuck outside the castle with him.

Both Edgar and James looked at her in horror. James spoke first, his tone urgent and pleading. "It's my fault, my king. I should have warned her about the consequences."

Edgar spoke through his clenched jaw. "We made a deal that you would behave, and you have already broken our agreement the same night we made it. What's worse is now one of my best soldiers knows about your magic."

James took a step forward. "Please, Your Majesty, I take full blame. You can punish me, not her."

Elice furrowed her eyebrows. She looked between James, his eyes wide with terror, and Edgar, his narrowed in anger. She knew she would get in some sort of trouble for using her magic—she knew what a ban was, after all—but it seemed as if she had missed something.

The king stood from his seat, his regal stature bearing down on them from where he stood, making Elice take a step backward. "This is now a family matter, Captain. Leave us."

James, still wide-eyed with fear, eased his way to the door, looking back at Elice with a worried expression.

As soon as the door shut, Edgar plopped into his chair. He buried his face in his hands and gave a pained groan.

Elice couldn't stand the quiet. "James was just being nice. He obviously had nothing to do with me using magic."

Her father lifted his hands away from his face. "Do you know what kind of position you've put me in?"

Elice swallowed at the grave tone in his voice. "I was just releasing some energy. I have to let out the energy my magic holds otherwise…" She didn't finish her explanation—would he even understand what she felt?

He groaned again. "I told you about the law. I warned you not to use your magic. No one is allowed to use magic."

"But it's just a dumb law created out of fear." Now she felt frustrated by this repeated insult against her and her powers.

"I created that law to keep everyone safe. There are people out there who share Orser's belief in the superiority of mages."

"Not every mage wants to hurt others. Besides, people without magic hurt others, too."

"That's not the point."

"It's exactly the point! Your fear of the past is blinding you of the future." Elice knew their voices carried out of the room and alerted others of their argument.

"I am the king! Everyone must obey my rules." Edgar slammed a fisted hand on the armrest.

"Well, I'm your daughter! But that doesn't seem to matter to you. You easily gave up on me, and now you want to marry me off to the first person who will have me."

Elice's entire body shook from the pressure of trying to keep her powers reigned in. Her fingernails dug into her palms, and tears threatened to fall from her eyes. She refused to look away from her father's face—she wanted him to know, to see, exactly what she felt. His eyes, once glazed over with anger, now softened with grief.

"I am a mage," she said, her lower lip trembling. "I have beautiful, wonderful, powerful magic. But I would never hurt anyone, not on purpose. My entire life, I've been told my magic is an abomination, but now I know that's not true. James saw the beauty my magic can create. He even touched it without getting hurt. He can see me for who I really am, but I can't say the same about you. If you can't accept me for who I am, then I shouldn't stay in this castle, and you don't deserve to call me your daughter."

She turned, ready to leave the palace for good. If she had to go back to living alone, then she would. She understood not everyone would see the beauty of her magic, but that didn't mean she had to accept what they thought. She now realized she needed to spend some time enjoying her magic for once.

"Elice, wait," her father called. She halted her steps, wondering if she should even turn around. She heard him blow out a deep breath. "Please, show me."

She whipped around to face him, her eyes wide in shock at his words. She never would have thought he would ask to see her magic.

He stood and walked toward her. Elice lifted her hand, calling for a little storm to form. This one was smaller than the one she showed James—she didn't want to lose control since her emotions were all over the place.

"It looks like a tornado," he said in awe, his eyes never leaving the wondrous creation in her hand.

She slowed the swirling winds so he could see the tiny waterspouts move around. "I use both air and water magic for this one. I haven't learned how to add all three of my powers into one spell yet."

Edgar huffed a laugh. "That's because there haven't been any mages before you who could control three elements." He stepped closer to her with a hesitant look as he reached his hand toward the storm.

She only nodded her head in response, unsure why he was interested in her magic now.

He laughed as the water rolled around his fingers, sliding across his hand. When he caught her eyes, it surprised her to see them glimmer with ... was that pride she saw reflected in them? She didn't know, as this was a new reaction for her.

With a smile, he pulled his hand away and wiped away the water on the front of his robe. "I will allow you to continue practicing your magic, as long as no one else sees you using it."

Elice bit her lip to keep from saying anything that might ruin the moment. To her surprise, he leaned in for an awkward hug. He held her with gentle arms for a moment, as if afraid he was doing too much. It was a nice gesture, so she brought her arms to his back and gave him a reassuring pat.

When he pulled away, he offered her his arm, and she smiled as she hooked her hand on his elbow. He led her out of the throne room, opening the door for her to pass through first.

Upon exiting, they met the anxious faces of Julice, Alice, and James.

The king gave a short laugh when he noticed James. "You're still here, Captain?" With a shake of his head, Edgar continued walking down the hall. The smile in his eyes let everyone know he was not angry.

Julice turned to Elice when the king left the hall. "By the Fates, Elice, what happened?"

Elice shrugged. She figured James had told her enough already. "He's letting me practice magic," she said, hoping that would satisfy her mother's question.

The captain stepped forward and held Elice's hands. "Thank the Fates. I was so worried."

"It's all right, James. Everything worked out."

"Yes, we're all relieved," said Julice. She touched James's shoulder and met his eyes. "Though we should all go to bed now. It's quite late."

James nodded, then pressed a faint kiss to Elice's knuckles before wishing them all goodnight and disappearing into the dark hallway.

Her mother bid the two girls goodnight as well and took off down the hall after him, leaving the two sisters to walk together toward their rooms.

Alice followed Elice into her suite and sat on the edge of her bed. "I can't believe what just happened," she muttered as she plopped down.

"Me neither," Elice responded. "Now I can practice magic whenever I want, as long as no one sees me. And Lenore will be here any day now, so I'll finally get the answers I need." She jumped on the bed and then sat with crossed legs.

Alice wore a slight frown as she turned to face her sister. "That's not what I meant. You broke the law and didn't get in trouble."

Elice burst out a laugh at her sister's confused expression. "That rule about magic is stupid, anyway."

Now Alice looked scandalized, her mouth dropping open and her hand coming to her mouth. "That doesn't matter. We were all worried you would face punishment. James even tried to take the blame and said he should have stayed in the room to convince Father it was his fault. He was getting ready to go back in when you two came out."

"What's the big deal? So I face a little time in the castle's prison. I'm sure Father wouldn't have me rot there forever." Elice grabbed one of the new pillows that Alice helped her order and hugged it.

"Prison?" Alice shook her head. "The punishment isn't imprisonment, Elice—it's death."

Elice sat with her mouth agape for several moments. It finally dawned on her why everyone reacted with so much fear. She remembered her father's words and how angry he seemed—not only because she used magic, but because of what he thought he had to do. After a moment, she closed her mouth and shook her head. "He didn't go through with the punishment, but I can't help feeling upset he even thought about it."

"Being a king means making hard decisions, Elice. I'm actually surprised at him."

"It shouldn't be about making only tough decisions—it should be about making the right decisions, too."

"It's always about tough choices." Alice looked at her with something akin to determination in her eyes, as if she were desperate for Elice to understand her point of view. "Right and wrong have nothing to do with it if someone breaks the law."

A scoff escaped Elice's mouth before she could stop it. "Sometimes there are bad laws, and if the law is wrong, then it should be changed. When you are queen, you can change the law whenever you see fit."

Alice turned away from her and sat in quiet for a moment. Then she stood from the bed. "I'm glad it seemed to have worked out for you," she muttered on her way to the door.

"If you were queen," Elice called out before Alice left the room, "what would you have done?" She didn't know if she should have asked that question, but the words forced their way out.

Alice paused with the door open before she whispered, "I don't know." She slipped through the door and closed it behind her.

Fourteen

Elice walked into Miss Tabitha's office right at eight, but the woman didn't acknowledge her promptness. She rushed Elice to the table and poured her some tea. With a gleam of curiosity in her eyes, she stared at her from across the table.

"The entire castle is talking about your late-night encounter with Lord Talin," the woman said, coming right out with it. She didn't even wait for Elice to take a sip of her tea, causing Elice to miss her mouth and spill the hot liquid over her dress.

"It wasn't like that," she muttered, wiping at her soiled dress with a napkin Miss Tabitha gave her.

The woman tilted her head. "Really?" she asked, drawing out the word.

Elice placed her cup on the table. She had rehearsed a half-truth all morning in case anyone approached her about it. "I was just taking a late-night stroll, and James happened to be there."

"Right." Tabitha gave her a knowing wink.

Elice ignored the woman's smirk. "I actually wanted to talk to you about something—it's a little personal."

Miss Tabitha blinked once, her own mug in danger of tipping over. "Of course, Your Highness." She sat straight in her chair and placed her teacup on the saucer.

Elice grabbed her tea again so she could have something to hold. "I took your advice and asked the king for closure, which I should get sometime soon."

"That's great, Princess," Miss Tabitha said with sincerity.

"But last night, something happened, and I don't know how to feel about it. My father actually hugged me—it was kind of awkward, but before that moment, I had felt unwanted, even unloved by him. Now, I don't know how to feel." Elice squirmed in her seat, unsure if she was being too personal with her family's governess. Miss Tabitha knew everything and everyone in the castle, but that didn't mean she cared to have intimate conversations with anyone.

The woman leaned over the table to pat Elice's hand. "It seems as if you can now have a proper relationship with your father."

Elice looked down at the woman's hand on top of her own. "How do you stay so strong and comfortable with who you are? I admire the way you remain so positive."

Miss Tabitha brought her hands over her heart, her eyes tearing up slightly. "Do you mean that?" When Elice nodded, the woman shook her head. "Most people seem to hate me, or, at the very least, they're annoyed by me. But I haven't become a successful governess by hiding who I am or running away from my problems. I suppose I just live my life the way the Fates made me—with smiles, positivity, and confidence."

"I want to be as confident as you are," Elice told her with a smile. She meant every word—she had recognized the woman's poise the moment she met her. Elice felt she had a lot of growing up to do, and she hoped to grow into a smart and courageous woman one day. To do that, she wanted to learn from as many women as she could—she made a mental note to have more talks with her mother, as well.

Miss Tabitha looked around at the table and, in one motion, pushed aside the various papers, lists, and swatches. "Why don't you choose what we do today?" she suggested.

Elice gave a sideways smile before she reached for the swatches and brought them close. Tabitha gave her a nod before they began discussing the details of her dress for the ball.

They remained that way for some time—sipping their tea and snacking on a few biscuits—until Alice appeared. Miss Tabitha had suggested they bring her into the conversation, though Elice held her tongue. She thought about Alice's refusal to answer her question the night before, and it made her wonder why her sister didn't take her side right away.

"You requested to see me, Miss Tabitha," she said as she entered the office. Elice noticed how Alice avoided making eye contact with her.

Miss Tabitha tapped the back of the chair closest to her. "Please sit down, Your Highness. I wanted to talk to you about Princess Elice's fabulous idea."

The woman continued after Alice sat. "She suggested that instead of wearing matching gowns, you both can choose your own dress. It's brilliant! You both have such different styles and personalities."

The corners of Alice's mouth turned down as she hummed in response.

"Princess Elice has already chosen hers—a sky-blue gown from the collection that would look just divine on her. You can choose yours now, and then we will summon the seamstress immediately for alterations."

Alice looked through the booklet Tabitha had set on the table in front of her. After perusing through the pages of in-stock gowns from the local dressmaker's shop, she decided on a light-yellow dress, as Elice expected.

"That's a beautiful color," Miss Tabitha proclaimed.

"Yellow's my favorite," Alice muttered, looking at her lap.

"Hmm," Tabitha hummed off-handedly as she scribbled a note. She left the room to find a maid who could summon the castle seamstress.

The two girls sat in uncomfortable silence. Alice refused to meet her sister's eyes, and Elice followed suit, still upset about the previous night.

After a long moment, Alice broke the silence. "I actually suggested we choose our own gowns in the beginning."

Elice looked at her sister, who had her gaze set on her hands in her lap. "Maybe she just didn't hear you," she offered, her resolve breaking as she looked upon her sister's somber mood.

Alice caught her eyes before she looked down again. "It's because no one listens to me as they do you."

With that, Alice stood and walked out the door without another word. When Miss Tabitha returned, she didn't acknowledge Alice's absence. She continued rattling on with enthusiasm about the changes they could make to the party. Elice, however, couldn't help the concern that washed over her when she thought about Alice's words.

～

To avoid running into James, Elice arrived at the shed earlier than she had on previous occasions. James, however, was already there when she walked in. He seemed as surprised as she was, judging by his wide-eyed look.

"I didn't think you'd be here this early," he said. He wiped his hands on the front of his uniform pants, making them dirty for the first time since Elice met him.

She stepped into the small space. "I didn't think you'd even come after last night, but I wanted to train early, just in case."

James closed the distance until they were standing close. "I just wanted to replenish your practice supplies and make it roomier in here."

Elice looked around the space and noticed he moved the small table to a corner, leaving more room to throw around her magic. She turned to James and placed her hands on her hips. "Why are you being so nice to me?"

Elice noticed the way his cheeks darkened with a blush as he smiled at her. Then, almost as if he remembered something, his face obscured with a serious, cloudy expression. "Remember when I said I knew of other mages? In Talin, I've tried to keep their powers secret. I've made it a priority back home to make sure no one gets caught if they've used their magic."

Elice lowered her arms and dug the toe of her soft shoe into the dirt. "You seem ... invested, somehow. Like it affects you."

James raked a hand across the top of his head. "There was someone from my village. She was a healer. When someone from a neighboring village suspected her of using magic... I couldn't protect her. Now, her daughter is without a mother."

Elice worked through the tightness in her throat. "She was executed? Because of my father's ridiculous law?"

He nodded, and his eyebrows scrunched close together. "I worried the same would happen to you. The Fates are on your side, I suppose."

"I don't know if the Fates had anything to do with it. All I know is, somehow, I'm going to convince my father to change the law." She set her jaw in determination. Ever since her conversation with Alice, she knew what she had to do—if no one else would change things for the better, then it was up to her. In her heart, she knew magic—even her own magic—was not inherently bad. Sure, she knew there were bad people out there, but that was true about everyone—regardless of whether they had magic.

James set his face as well and, to Elice's surprise, he bowed before her, holding her hand and once again pressing one of his gentle kisses upon it. "I offer my services to you on your mission, my princess."

Elice chuckled as he stood straight again, placing his hands, one over the other, above his heart in the traditional sign of respect. "Please," she said, exasperated, "just call me Elice."

He shook his head. "I have too much respect for you to degrade your title."

Elice couldn't help but roll her eyes. Then she remembered something else she wanted to discuss with him, which made her shuffle her feet again. "About the party—about the whole..." She moved her hands in a circle between them—she didn't know what to call it. Were they really engaged?

To her relief, he continued for her as if he understood her hand motions. "I expect nothing other than to accompany you to your first ball. I take it your parents threw you into this without asking you."

"My parents didn't even tell me about it. Miss Tabitha was the one who let it slip about an engagement."

"I'm sorry. I hope this won't make you feel uncomfortable around me."

"I'm not uncomfortable," she blurted, though she didn't quite meet his eyes. "I just want you to know where I stand on the whole engagement thing. It's not something I'm thinking about, and I don't want you to take things the wrong way."

He nodded and said, "I understand."

Sensing his hesitation, she reached out and nudged his shoulder, bringing a soft smile to her lips. "I also don't want you to feel uncomfortable around me. After all, you're the only person outside my family who knows I'm a mage. I would hate to lose my only friend."

"My princess," he said, giving her hand a squeeze. "If you want a friend, then that's exactly what I'll be for you."

She was happy he could be a friend to her—though she ignored the way her heart dropped an inch in her chest. Did she want to be just friends with James? She didn't know, but at least they could remain this way until she figured it out.

∾

After spending some time in the shed, she strutted back to her room without fear of running into a guard. She had the king's permission, barring anyone catching her using magic, to be outside her room at any given moment, no matter how late. She opened the door to her suite and walked to her bedroom. As soon as she opened the second door, a shadowy movement caught her by surprise, making her jump backward into the door.

"Elice?" her sister whispered.

She sighed in relief and calmed her breathing, lowering her hands and releasing the wind she had prepared to strike with. "Yes, it's me. By the Fates, you scared me. What are you doing in my room, alone, in the dark?"

Alice walked over to the side table and lit the candle that rested in its golden holder. "Were you in the shed?" she asked, ignoring Elice's question.

Elice lifted her chin as she answered a quick, "Yes."

"Was James there?" Alice met her eyes, holding the contact as she studied Elice's expression.

"He was already there to rearrange some things, but he left right away." Elice crossed her arms, a frown forming on her face. She didn't know why she felt the need to explain herself—her father had already given her permission to practice, and he never said she couldn't see James anymore.

Alice stepped closer to her sister, remaining an arm's length away. "I'm sorry about the other night. You're my sister, and no matter what, I'll always love you. I don't want us to waste any time being upset with each other or to think we don't care about each other."

Elice looked at her sister, who stood with her fingers twisting and wringing as if they were roots digging deep into the ground. A part of her still burned with anger as she thought about Alice's hurtful words, but a larger part yearned to make up with her and tell her everything was all right. "I don't want to fight with you, either. You're right; we're finally together after all this time, so we shouldn't waste any time arguing."

They smiled at each other before they closed the distance for a hug. As Elice placed her head on her sister's shoulder, she realized she didn't want to waste time on negative feelings. While it still upset her, she pushed the anger away and gripped her sister tighter.

The girls stayed up a few extra minutes, sitting crisscrossed on the bed and holding pillows in their laps while Elice told her exactly what happened last night with James and their father. Alice's eyes seemed glued open, and Elice worried her sister forgot to breathe as she recounted her story. When she finally finished, Elice shook her sister's shoulder to snap her out of it.

Alice drew in a deep breath. "Well, I'm really glad that's over."

"The story or the event?" Elice titled her head to the side.

"Both."

The girls rolled over in laughter, gripping their pillows as they flopped onto their backs.

Alice turned her head to look at her sister. "In all seriousness, please stop getting into trouble. I can't take any more of this action."

Elice smirked. "I make no promises."

Alice rolled her eyes before she threw the pillow at Elice's face, causing both girls to laugh again.

"All right," Alice said in between breaths, "I give up. I'm going to bed."

Elice stuck her tongue out and threw a pillow toward her, but Alice slammed the door before it made contact. As Elice stared at the closed door, she could hear her twin's laughter.

With a smile on her face, she rolled out of bed and began changing into a nightgown so she could finally get some sleep.

The next morning, while she sat and listened to Miss Tabitha's gossip, it surprised her to see Alice join them.

"Ah, Princess Alice," Tabitha said. "Now that you're here, we can head to the ballroom for our group lesson. There are only three days left until the big day, so we must use what little time we have."

Elice groaned. "Why are we going to the ballroom?"

The woman waved a hand at her. "Don't pretend you're not eager to dance with James again." She gave her a wink before they walked out of the office.

"James will be there?" She ignored the way her cheeks heated at the mention of his name.

"Of course, Princess. It's a group session—we must practice the grand entrance."

Elice didn't like how that sounded.

Not long after they entered the ballroom, Andre sauntered in through the wooden double doors. "Ladies," he said with his usual gusto, flourishing his arms to either side like he was giving the air a hug.

Just as he lowered his arms, James appeared behind him. He walked past without acknowledging Andre and went straight to Alice, giving her a bow. "Princess Alice, it's so good to see you again." She pulled him into a hug, which he returned. They both closed their eyes and gave one last squeeze before letting go. When he made his way to Elice, he gave her a tender kiss on the hand. "My princess. How are you this morning?"

"Fine," Elice croaked out.

Miss Tabitha cleared her throat, breaking Elice's eye contact with him. The woman winked at her again before calling the group to order.

Elice noticed the boys refused to say anything to each other, but she wouldn't be the one to point out that fire in the room. She didn't know the extent of their relationship, or the lack thereof. However, by the way Andre side-eyed James, she knew to avoid it at all costs—she wasn't in the mood to cause any trouble, at least not about this.

Standing in front of the grand staircase, Miss Tabitha faced the group. "Now, the grand entrance is the most critical moment of the entire night. It is the first impression you will give your guests—especially for you, my dear Princess Elice, seeing as this is your first introduction to high society. So, this lesson is primarily for you, since your sister has done a grand entrance several times now."

Elice stood still and blinked at Tabitha, trying to understand what she meant. "So ... you want me to..." she trailed off, leaving the words hanging in the air.

Andre snickered from his place at the end of the line, which made Miss Tabitha roll her eyes. "You will practice walking down the grand staircase where, at the bottom, your escort will graciously hold out his hand for you and lead you out onto the ballroom floor."

Elice stammered for a moment, trying to find the words to express her apprehension. "I'm not sure how I feel about being in such a big spotlight."

"You will be fine, Princess. Princess Alice will go first to show you how it's done."

As if on cue, Alice turned and walked up the steps, one hand holding the railing while the other lifted the hem of her dress so she didn't trip on her way up. At the top, she twirled around and descended—just as slow and graceful as her ascent. Andre waited in his dedicated spot by the end of the railing. He brandished his hand, and Alice placed her hand gingerly in his.

"There," Miss Tabitha said, clapping. She turned to Elice and motioned toward Alice. "That's how you do it. Now it's your turn."

Elice gripped her sister's arm. "Wait, can you do it again, Alice?" she begged.

Tabitha gave her a light push in the direction of the stairs. "It's not that bad. It's easier than you think."

"What if I trip?" Elice halted at the bottom of the stairs, looking up at the long flight before her. She had not yet gotten used to wearing heels and long dresses, especially when combined with stairs.

"You won't," Miss Tabitha said with another push. "But if you do, Lord Talin will surely catch you."

Elice shot him a desperate look, her eyes asking if he really would catch her if she fell. James ducked his head as he tried to hide a laugh, which didn't assure Elice of his intent to catch her.

She made her way up the stairs. It wasn't a graceful trip like Alice's since she walked with clumsy, wide steps, but she thanked the Fates she didn't fall. Once at the top, she took a shaky first step, looking down at her feet as she went. Her curls fell and covered her face, so she lifted the hand holding the rail to brush a thick strand behind her ear.

Just as she returned her hand to the rail, the same curl released itself from its hold and blocked her face again. Elice groaned but continued walking down the staircase, even though her field of vision seemed to minimize with each step.

When she was a few steps away from the bottom, she swept her hair away again, this time using the hand holding onto her dress. Her shoe snagged on the front hem, causing her to lose her footing.

Her eyes slammed shut in fear of the fall down the last few steps. Air rushed to her fingers, asking her if she needed help. She wanted to accept its offer and blast a column of air to push herself upright, but she felt sturdy arms wrap around her waist and pull her into an embrace. She spun in midair, both she and her savior twisting as they gripped each other tightly. Their bodies came to a stop, one of his hands gripping her arm and the other snaking around her back.

Elice opened her eyes and met James's chocolate brown ones.

He was bent over her as he desperately held her above the ground. Her breathing became laborious as she realized she had tripped and almost used her magic in front of Miss Tabitha. She doubted her father would have forgiven her, since Miss Tabitha was the biggest gossip in the castle.

She swallowed and tried to find her breath. "Thank you."

James tucked a loose strand of curls behind her ear. "You really didn't think I would let you fall, did you?"

A warmth spread across her face, and she knew she was blushing. Someone cleared their throat—a deep rumble that sounded like it came from Andre—and Elice broke her eye contact to find everyone staring at her and James. With his help, she stood and walked down the last step.

Miss Tabitha cut the awkward silence with a round of applause. "Well, that was exciting. Let's run it again, shall we? Up you go, Princess Elice. Try not to trip this time."

Elice rolled her eyes, but did what Miss Tabitha asked—this time, she made it all the way down without falling. She practiced her grand entrance several more times before Tabitha called an end to that lesson, satisfied that she could walk down the stairs the way she needed to.

Just when Elice thought their practice session would end, Miss Tabitha had them practicing their opening group waltz. "You will run through the dance steps until I'm satisfied the four of you are completely in sync," she said before clapping her hands. As if by magic, the three violinists—Elice scrunched her nose, wondering if they lived in the castle for a reason she couldn't fathom—sauntered into the ballroom and struck up the opening number.

They were not in sync with each other, and Tabitha had them dancing for over two hours until she decided they could stop.

"Now, I want you all to remember the steps," Tabitha said. "I have much work to do over the next two days, so I will expect you to practice on your own." She gave Elice a pointed look.

Elice shrugged as the group walked away from the dance floor.

James, walking beside her, whispered, "Perhaps I'll see you tonight?"

Alice and Andre turned their heads in her direction, having heard the captain's words. Elice bit the inside of her lip and nodded to keep from squeaking out a response.

At the door, he kissed her hand again before wishing Alice and Miss Tabitha a good day. Andre's glare went unnoticed by James as the captain walked right past him on his way out.

"I hope you actually get some rest tonight, Princess Elice," Miss Tabitha said from behind her. Elice left the room before anyone could see her blush again.

Fifteen

When she arrived at the shed that night, she stood at the doorway, staring inside the space. At first, she thought James would show up later, so she began practicing. As the night continued, she realized he wouldn't come.

Her magic distracted her, yet there were a few moments when she wondered why she cared whether he showed up. Wasn't she the one who needed space and wanted to be just friends? Elice nodded to herself as she cleaned up the shed after she finished for the night. It was better if they stopped these late-night meetings, she told herself. She didn't want him to get the wrong idea.

She thought about it all the way back to her room, and even in the morning when she met Miss Tabitha, she couldn't help but think how James had stood her up. He was the one who had suggested they talk again that night, and he didn't even bother to show up.

Miss Tabitha must have noticed her sour mood because she sent her to the library right away with a large notebook to read. The notebook had a guest list detailing which city each guest was from, what their line of work was, and why they were an important member of society. Miss Tabitha told her to memorize all this information in just two days.

It took ten minutes for restlessness to settle in. Elice told herself she would only stand up to stretch her legs and then she would continue studying, but she ended up wandering away from the library. Before she realized it, she stood in front of the barrack's main entrance.

With resolve, she set her jaw and walked into the building closest to her. It was a maze of metal halls and unrecognizable doors. The doors themselves had plaques indicating who the room belonged to or what was stored inside. As she wandered around, she noticed most rooms were living quarters.

Soldiers hurried about with purpose. Elice thought about asking someone for help, but they all seemed too busy and she didn't recognize a single face. After another turn around a corner, she found what she was looking for: Captain James Taylor's office. She raised a hand to knock when someone popped up beside her.

"May I help you, Your Highness?" said a man in a formal tone.

She looked at the soldier who had appeared beside her. He was tall and muscular, and she guessed he was in his late twenties.

"Yes, I'm looking for Captain Taylor," she said.

"The captain isn't here at the moment. He returned to Talin last night."

Elice blinked in surprise. "Oh, thank you," she said before she turned to leave. She was shocked to hear that James had returned home with only two days left until the party. Was he planning on standing her up again? A flood of unease filled her, making her stomach clench as she thought about not having a date to her party after all she'd gone through the past few days just to have one.

She stopped in her tracks when she realized she might have scared him away by making it seem like she wasn't interested in him. Then she shook her head—she didn't know if she was interested or not, but that shouldn't stop him from keeping his promise to her. Besides, he said he wanted to be friends with her even if they weren't engaged.

Elice started for the library when a familiar voice caught her attention. She peeked down the next hallway and saw Andre walking toward her, flanked by the same two soldiers he always seemed to be around.

She was not in the mood to talk to him, but he had already noticed her. Since it now seemed impossible to avoid him, she straightened and waited for him in the middle of the hall.

"Good morning, Lord Copita," she said and then nodded at the other two. They gave her a respectful bow before Andre signaled their dismissal with a nod of his own.

"What brings you into the barracks on such a beautiful day?" he asked in his usual high energy.

"I was actually looking for James." She caught the uncomfortable look that flashed across his face at the mention of James's name.

"You mean he didn't tell you?" Andre raised an eyebrow and then shook his head. "He left for Talin immediately after Miss

Tabitha's lesson. Apparently, he received an urgent letter. I was sure he would tell you since it's such a long trip there and back. He might not make it back in time for the party."

Elice looked at her feet, an uncomfortable feeling sinking into the pit of her stomach.

Andre stepped closer. "I warned you not to trust him, Elice. I don't want to see you get hurt."

She didn't know what to say to him. Was he right to warn her? Should she be wary of the feelings that stirred in her stomach and the blushes that warmed her cheeks when she thought about James?

He sighed at her silence. "You probably don't want to hear it, and it's probably wrong of me to say, but I care about you. Ever since I first met you, I haven't been able to stop thinking about you."

Elice drew in a sharp inhale and snapped her eyes to his. She knew he was an overly passionate person, but she never expected this kind of confession to come from him. At her continued silence, Andre sighed once more and then walked down the hallway behind her.

After a moment, she turned to leave the same way and almost ran into a small group of soldiers. How long had they been standing there?

Embarrassed and wondering how much they heard, she stormed past them, ignoring their whispers. It was only a matter of time before the entire palace caught wind of her conversation with Andre.

Hiding out in the library seemed a good plan, even if she had homework from Miss Tabitha. When she returned, she sat in the back of the extensive room at the bench she now deemed her special spot.

She resumed her studies, reading name after name, description after description, and making a mental note of everything. It reminded her of reading from her usual boring books back in the cottage when she had nothing better to do with her time.

The sun fell low on the horizon, and the breeze outside welcomed her tired mind. Sighing, she lifted a hand and played with the current that drifted through the open window. With her mind finally relaxed, she almost missed the sound of footsteps. She peeked around the bookshelf to find Alice walking toward her.

"Are you going to hide in here all day?" Alice asked as she sat on the bench beside her.

Elice wanted to groan aloud. "Is there gossip already?"

Alice made a noncommittal noise. "You're only popular because you're new to everyone. It'll die down, eventually."

"In the meantime, I think I'll hide out in the library." To emphasize her point, she lifted the notebook.

"If it makes you feel better, I haven't heard too many people talking about your run-in with Dre."

Elice lowered her head to the desk, slamming her forehead on the hard wood. "I'd rather not listen to it—or talk about it."

"People were talking about my engagement as soon as it was announced, but they forgot soon enough. Trust me; they will grow bored with you. In the meantime, perhaps try to walk a ... quieter path?"

Elice turned her head to the side on the table and squinted her eyes, but laughed when Alice gave a smile. Her sister's innocent nature would always brighten her mood.

~

Dinner couldn't have passed quickly enough. Elice mostly avoided eye contact with everyone at the table, pushing around the food on her plate without really eating much of it. To her surprise, Andre stayed rather quiet as well. He answered the king's questions with fewer words than normal and without his usual gusto.

Julice caught her eye, and Elice wondered if her mother could read minds because the woman's face took on a knowing expression. The woman pursed her lips but didn't push for conversation. She likely heard about Elice's newest escapade with another member of the nobility.

Edgar drank from his wine and talked too much, giving Elice the impression he either ignored gossip or didn't actually hear it. Either way, Elice thanked the Fates she didn't have to talk about Andre's feelings for her.

Elice wanted to roll her eyes at how stereotypical all this turned out to be. She never asked for the attention she received, and she wanted to run away from it all.

Her mother, however, had other plans.

Julice came knocking on her door after Elice retired to her room. Elice wished she could just hide in her bedchamber, avoiding the public and balls forever. She even asked the Fates for a prison cell, especially when her mother entered the room and gave her a fierce look.

"I can explain," Elice began as soon as Julice placed her hands on her hips.

"Please do," Julice said before she crossed the room and sat on the edge of the bed.

Elice sat next to her with a plop. "Well, I can't really explain."

"Elice," her mother said in a warning tone.

"But it's only because I don't fully understand it." Elice reached for the nearest pillow to squeeze.

Julice sighed and grabbed the pillow from Elice's arms. "You'll need to do better than that. The entire castle is talking about you and Andre. Please tell me it's not true."

"That depends on what people are saying..."

Upon seeing her mother's glare—a softer version of Lenore's, Elice noted thankfully—she hurried through a shortened recount of what happened, including all the times Andre had flirted with her. Elice's embarrassment made her cheeks overheat and her palms sweat, but once she started talking to her mother about it, she realized she felt better.

"The thing is," Elice said, "I don't think I feel the same way about him. Sure, he's funny and incredibly handsome, but he's engaged to Alice. Even if he weren't, though, I don't feel..."

"Warm and cozy inside," Julice finished for her, passing her the soft pillow with a slight smirk.

Elice brought the pillow to her chest again and held it tight. "But James, he's so different from Dre."

Julice laughed as Elice sighed softly. "I definitely believe that." They shared a knowing smile before Julice's face became serious once more. "How does Alice feel about all of this? I'm sure she's heard about it."

Elice grimaced and looked away. "Oh, she knows. She just doesn't love Dre that way, either."

A perfectly sculpted eyebrow raised on Julice's forehead. Before Julice could ask another question, Elice forced out a large yawn, hoping to avoid having to explain Alice's own messed-up love life to their mother.

"I'm exhausted, Mother. I think I'll go to bed now." To emphasize her point, Elice crawled underneath her covers and faced the opposite wall.

Julice reached over and swept some of the curls from Elice's face, gently tucking them behind her ear. "Goodnight, then," Julice whispered and gave one last pat to Elice's head before she left the room.

The next morning, Elice went straight to the library with her guest list. After she settled on her cushioned bench and dove into her reading, the doors to the library opened. She couldn't hold back the groan that escaped—she had closed the doors with the hope that anyone passing by might overlook the library for the day and not bother her. Lifting the notebook, she tried to cover her face in a poor attempt to conceal herself.

"Princess, are you in here?" James' voice called to her from the front of the library.

Elice sat up in her seat, heart racing as she wondered whether she wanted to see James at the moment. She took a deep breath, resolving not to be afraid to face him—or anyone—ever again. She had already spent too much time living in fear.

Yet, as his footsteps grew closer, she hadn't made a move to respond to him.

He appeared at the end of the row, dressed in his crisp uniform buttoned all the way to the top. He smiled upon seeing her, and the sight of it threatened to calm her anger at being stood up by him.

"I've been looking for you," he said as he made his way to the small table in front of her. "Miss Tabitha said I might find you in here."

"I've been studying," she muttered, looking down at her notebook.

"I returned early this morning, and I wanted to stop by and say hello." His smile wavered when she only nodded her reply and continued reading. "Is ... everything all right?"

She looked up from her book at the tone in his voice. Managing her displeasure became easier once she saw the way his eyebrows furrowed on his puzzled face. She breathed a quiet breath to calm her nerves, which always seemed to fluctuate around him. "I didn't think you'd be back so quickly. I didn't even know you left."

"You didn't know?" His frown made Elice pout along with him as she shook her head. "I wrote you a note as soon as I found out I was needed in Talin."

She lowered her notebook to the desk. "I never got a note."

James motioned to the bench, asking permission to sit, and Elice scooted over to make room for him. "You waited for me that night." His words didn't sound like a question, so she didn't answer. "And you went to look for me in the morning but ran into Andre instead."

She stared at him, her eyes unblinking as she tried to gauge his reaction. Apparently he had heard about her meeting with Andre already. She had hoped he would never hear about Andre confessing he couldn't stop thinking about her. Elice couldn't decide how she felt about it, so knowing that James knew made her fidget in her seat.

James clasped his hands together on his lap. "One of my men told me you came looking for me and that you had an encounter with Andre. I'm not surprised he has feelings for you. I'm just worried about you and your sister."

"She knows," Elice said, then cringed at the reality of the situation. It felt so wrong to be in the middle of it. "Besides, she's in love with someone else."

He nodded, wringing his fingers together. "So, you and Andre are…"

"Nothing," she finished, "we're not anything—and I have no intention of changing that."

There was an awkward silence as they sat on the bench together. Elice cleared her throat to break the tension before she asked what was on her mind. "What happened to the note you wrote to me?"

"I don't know. I gave it to my aide to deliver to the mailroom. Usually, the pages are prompt, but it could've gotten lost on its way to you."

"Andre seemed to know you had to leave right after Miss Tabitha's lesson. Was he nearby when you found out you had to leave?"

James's eyes narrowed, but he nodded. "He was behind me when my aide came rushing up with news from my estate."

"Did he know you were going to send me a note?" Elice crossed her arms as she thought about Andre somehow stopping the note from getting to her. His angry glares at the back of James's head flashed in her mind.

"I'm sure he heard me say I would write to you, but I don't like where this train of thought is going. I don't want to think he would somehow sabotage my letter."

Elice shrugged. "Well, I guess you know him better than I do."

James pointed to the forgotten notebook on the table and changed the subject. "What are you studying?"

"The guest list." Elice pulled the notes closer.

"I can help you, since I'm sure I know most of the people on the list."

Elice's eyes lit up. "You would help me? Because this is almost as boring as sitting alone in my cottage all day."

"I don't have any plans today as important as helping you, my princess."

They leaned over the notebook and spent the better part of an hour reviewing everything she needed to learn by tomorrow night.

~

"You asked for me, Your Highness?" Serena stood by the door and gave Elice a curtsey.

"I need your help, Serena." Elice waved for her maid to come inside, and the girl closed the door behind her.

Serena's eyes grew wide before she remembered herself and lowered them. "Of course. I'm happy to be of service."

Elice ignored the girl's enthusiasm. It was the first time she asked for Serena's help, but she knew they had different definitions of the word 'help.' "Do you know anything about a letter from Captain Taylor addressed to me?"

Again, Serena's eyes widened as she stammered unintelligible words.

Elice walked to the girl and placed a gentle arm on her shoulder. "It's all right. No one's going to get in trouble. I just need to know what happened."

Serena hesitated, but answered in a quiet voice. "I heard something about a letter for you."

Elice knew it was right to ask her maid—Miss Tabitha once said she learned all the good gossip from the servants. "I never got it. Do you happen to know why?"

The young girl nodded. "I don't want to get anyone in trouble."

"I told you; no one's getting in trouble." Elice patted the girl's shoulder.

After a deep breath, she muttered, "I heard the person who was supposed to deliver the letter was ordered not to."

Elice scrunched her eyes. "Do you know who gave the order?"

Serena shook her head. "I don't know. I only know the page was worried he would lose his job if he didn't do what he was told."

"Thank you, Serena." Elice smiled at her. "Where can I find the page who was supposed to deliver my letter?"

Serena told her the location of the mail room, then gave her the name and description of the person.

Elice exited the castle and walked to a modest-sized building by the stables, where she saw couriers coming and going. The mail room was more like a large shed with two doors on opposite sides of the building—one for entering, the other for exiting. She entered the structure and saw the young man she was looking for. He wore a brown cap over his thick dark hair and a brown vest, the pockets of which were stuffed with envelopes and sheets of paper.

When he looked up from the table of envelopes, their eyes met, and he froze. Elice sauntered over, doing her best not to let her eyes wander—she wanted him to know she meant business.

"I am Elice of House Moore, Princess of Norraine." She tried her best to sound like Alice. Instead, she appeared loud and absurd to her own ears. However, judging by the panicked look on his face, it had the intended effect, so she continued. "We haven't met before, but I know who you are, and now you know who I am. As I'm sure you know, we have something to discuss."

Without waiting for a response, she turned and walked out the exit door, sure he would follow. As soon as she exited, he came out right behind her. Elice smiled and closed the door.

"Let's get straight to it, shall we?" She leaned against the door to make sure no one else walked through it, and it gave her an unobstructed view of the path behind him. There was enough privacy since no one except the couriers would come this way and she was blocking the only exit. "I know what you were asked to do, so that makes this easy. I only have two questions for you. No one needs to get in trouble here, but the king would be very upset if he heard about this."

She didn't know if her father would even care about her current predicament, but the courier didn't need to know that. "My first question is: who ordered you not to deliver my letter from Lord Talin?"

The courier pulled the hat from his head and fumbled with it. "Lord Copita, Your Highness."

Elice breathed deep, feeling struck down by his answer yet determined not to waver. "Now, my second question: where is the letter now?"

He gave her a pitiful look, his eyes pleading and his bottom lip quivering. "In the garbage bins behind the stables."

Elice set her jaw as she thought about the state her letter was in. "Well, I suppose you should hurry and get it." He hesitated for only a moment before he took off, running away from her like she was spewing fire magic at him. She paced behind the door, ignoring the few pages who exited and gave her questioning looks as they passed.

When he returned, he held the letter—covered in bits of rotting food and dirt. She took it, happy to have it, yet disgusted at the same time.

She had one more stop to make before she went back inside the castle. Lucky for her, she knew Andre's routine by now. Since the sun would soon set, he would head to his room in the barracks to get ready for dinner with her family.

Andre stopped short of his door as soon as he saw her leaning against it, filthy letter in hand. His eyes narrowed in on it before he lifted his hands out in defense. "I can explain—"

Elice pushed off the door, cutting him off with no regard for who might be nearby to hear her. "I trusted you. I thought you were my friend."

"I am your friend, Elice. You have to understand—"

"You're just a spoiled, rich lord who thinks he can get away with anything. You say you care about me, but you only care about yourself." She pushed past him, too upset to finish what she came to say. It didn't matter, anyway, she told herself as she rushed out of the barracks. Her feelings were too confusing, and she didn't need to think about them. Not when she had a grimy letter from James to read.

She hurried to Alice's suite, the tears in her eyes making it hard to see more than a few feet in front of her. When she burst through the door, she shut it and leaned her back against it, gasping for breath as she steadied herself.

"Elice, are you all right?" came Alice's voice as she poked her head into the parlor. Elice wiped her eyes with the back of her hand.

"I'm fine—better now." She held the envelope for her sister to see.

Alice scrunched up her face in disgust. "What in the Fates' names is that?"

"A letter from James." Elice walked into Alice's bedroom and jumped on the bed, lying on her stomach as she opened the letter.

"Do I want to know why it smells like garbage?" Alice mimicked her position on the bed.

"Nope," was Elice's distracted reply before she began reading aloud.

"My Princess,

I hope you are smiling as you read this note, because I have sudden news. My mother arrived in Talin and requested my immediate presence. I had wished to meet with you tonight to watch more of your beautiful magic. Alas, I won't get to see you for another day.

Please forgive my absence, but know I will return in time to meet you at the bottom of the grand staircase on your big day.

Your devoted friend,

J."

Elice folded the note and looked up to see Alice's smirk. She raised an eyebrow—she'd never seen Alice smirk, and the sight made her burst out in laughter. Soon, both girls were giggling on the bed, enjoying this moment of girlish sisterhood. Elice tried not to think about how they would be eighteen in another year, and no longer considered girls. They were growing into women, but for now, they could take pleasure in being young.

Sixteen

Miss Tabitha bounced around like a raging fire. Elice knew the servants wanted to avoid her, but they all feared she would yell at them if they went missing, even for a moment. So they remained close by her, fixing last minute issues or changing things Tabitha deemed wouldn't work for the ball.

Elice hid in the library for most of the day, still reviewing the notebook of guests, until Serena came to find her. It was finally time to get ready.

That's when her nerves got the better of her. Serena and four other maids engaged her in conversation, asking if she was excited or if she researched enough, but Elice merely responded with nods or quick answers. Her hands became sweaty whenever she thought about all the people she would soon meet, and her throat grew dry. Serena offered to bring water, but Elice shook her head, afraid to put anything in her stomach in case she couldn't hold it in.

"You look beautiful," Serena said with a smile as she finished setting her hair. Elice told her she wanted to look as natural as possible, so the girl kept the make-up and hairstyle simple. Her hair cascaded naturally down her back, a few pins holding back some of the curls by her face, and then it all came to rest gracefully by her hips.

Elice stood on shaky legs in front of the mirror, taking in the powder-blue gown with short, capped shoulders. The bodice hugged her tight all the way to her hips, where it flared out into a bell shape thanks to a thick layer of tulle underneath the skirt. On her feet, she wore soft white slippers with only a small heel. She swept her eyes higher again, catching the glint from Lenore's necklace, this time hanging above her gown for all to see.

Serena stood behind her and slid a few strands of hair to the front of Elice's shoulders. "There, now you're ready to go," she said.

Serena turned and opened the door. The other maids waved and wished her luck. Elice nodded and gave a shy half-smile. She walked out of her room in silence, following her maid to the second-floor chamber that led to the top of the grand staircase. That would be where she made her first entrance to high society.

Only two people stood waiting—the herald who would announce her arrival and one of Miss Tabitha's aides. The aide rushed to her as soon as she entered the room. "Your Highness, thank the Fates. Miss Tabitha expected you several minutes ago. Princess Alice just entered the room. Everyone is waiting for you now."

Elice's eyes widened, and she looked at Serena, who still accompanied her. Serena gave her a quick nod, but Elice shook her head.

In the back of her mind, she knew that if she hurried, she could leave the room before it was too late. She could hide in the library or perhaps out by the stables. No one would think to look for her there.

She looked down at her flowing blue gown—it was too long to run in, but if she kicked off the heels, she could make it work.

Before she could settle on her escape plan, Miss Tabitha burst through the door, causing Elice to jump.

"There you are," Tabitha yelled. "The people are getting restless."

"I can't do this," Elice whispered, her voice quivering and high-pitched.

Tabitha took in Elice's nervous state. With a forceful wave and shooing noise, she ordered everyone from the room. Serena and the aide stepped outside into the hallway while the herald turned away toward the curtain that led to the balcony. "My dear, what's the matter?" Tabitha grabbed her by the shoulders and gave her a little shake.

"I'm going to embarrass myself. I'll trip going down the stairs, or I'll say the wrong thing like I always do. What if I call a prominent lord by the wrong name or insult someone's business? Mother and Father will never want to look at me again. We're finally getting along, and I'm going to ruin it all. I just know it."

Miss Tabitha let all the air expire from Elice's rant before she spoke. "Do you really think that, Your Highness?" Elice bit her lip, but the woman didn't give her enough time to answer. "You've been hidden away all your life. Do you really want to go back to being that lonely, forgotten, lost little girl? Because when I look at you, beautiful ball gown or not, I see a young woman who deserves to shine. The question is: are you ready to take your rightful place in this world?" Tabitha gave her shoulder a light squeeze and left the room so Elice could process her words.

Elice closed her eyes. She didn't want to go back to the abandoned cottage in the forest—it wasn't an option anymore now that she had a taste of the real world. This, however, was not what she ever expected—to be a princess, to attend royal balls, to wear gorgeous gowns, and to dance long into the night with a handsome lord.

Yet, as she thought about the past two weeks of her life, she had done more in that brief time than she had in all her seventeen years of life combined. Was she ready to become a member of this grand royal world? She didn't know, but she knew in her heart that she wanted to find out.

With a shuddery breath, she walked to the curtain that separated the small room from the balcony in the grand ballroom. The herald stood at attention and saluted her with his hand over his heart. She nodded in reply, and he pulled the curtain to the side.

With a booming voice, he called out to the ballroom. "Introducing: Elice of House Moore. Princess of Norraine. Youngest daughter of His Royal Highness, King Edgar the Defender, and Her Royal Highness, Queen Julice of House Newton."

Another deep breath. She stepped onto the white marbled balcony and placed her left hand on top of the polished wooden banister, painted a bright white that reflected all the light from the candles that shined around her. She blinked several times before her eyes adjusted.

There were murmurs from the crowd, but she couldn't understand any of it. Instead, she focused on her breathing and steps as she used her free hand to grab the side of her dress, lifting it enough to descend the stairs without falling.

She counted the steps as she went, each number resounding in her head. As she turned the slight corner of the staircase, her eyes landed on James, and she almost faltered. She had never seen him outside of his uniform—the usual drab outfit with a matching hat. Tonight, he wore a sophisticated tuxedo fitted to showcase his muscular form. He had a crisp white shirt underneath his black coat, a black bow tie fastened under the collar, and a blue and white handkerchief in his left pocket that complemented her gown. There was even a blue lapel pin in the shape of a flower attached to the trim of his coat.

His smile was radiant as she descended, causing a smile of her own to form. She only had eyes for him and his outstretched hand. When she made it to the last step, she placed her hand in his. He bowed and placed a slow kiss on her hand.

Her heart raced as he guided her to the middle of the dance floor, where Alice and Andre stood waiting with their arms in the proper stance for their dance. Elice spun in place to face James, and after four heartbeats, the high-pitched whine of the violins echoed throughout the ballroom. Not losing eye contact, they began their waltz, dancing with each other in time to the couple next to them. She couldn't look away from James, though she could feel Alice's and Andre's presence as they all glided along the polished floor.

It went as practiced, and Elice couldn't believe how well she danced. At the end of the song, the couples pulled away from each other and the two young men bowed low before the princesses. That signaled applause and the point at which other couples could join them on the dance floor.

As soon as the next song began and James stood upright, Elice, still buzzing with the thrill of her emotions, threw herself into his arms and wrapped her arms around his neck. "I can't believe I didn't mess up," she shouted over the sound of music and conversation.

James pulled away enough to look her in the eyes. "You were great! I knew you could do it." He had to raise his voice to be heard over the commotion of the party.

Elice grinned as she lowered her arms and grabbed his hands. "I couldn't have done it without you."

They walked through the crowd of people now taking over the floor. When they emerged, her father and mother greeted them.

Queen Julice wiped away tears, but wore a soft smile. "My daughter," she said as she extended her hand for Elice's. "I'm so proud."

Elice's throat constricted as she soaked in her mother's warm adoration. They held hands for a long moment before her father cut in.

"You look wonderful tonight, dear," he said, and there was a glint in his eyes as he looked at her.

"Thank you," she whispered. All this attention would take some getting used to. James bowed to the king and queen, but her father reached out and shook his hand.

An elderly couple dressed in a coordinating gray suit and dress approached and bowed before them.

"Lord Gref. Lady Gref." Edgar greeted the man with a hand over his heart before turning to the woman and giving her the same salute. "I would like to introduce you to my youngest daughter, Princess Elice."

Elice peered at James from the corner of her eye, who gave her an encouraging nod. "Lord Gref, and Lady Gref, it's so nice to meet you." She held out her hand, as Miss Tabitha taught her, and they took turns holding it in a gentle grasp. She recalled what she knew about the village of Gref and the lord and lady before her. "I haven't had the pleasure of visiting Gref, but I look forward to making a trip there in the future. It's been a dream of mine to attend the springtime festival. I know how proud the citizens of Gref are of their hard work in decorating the town for the celebration."

The two nobles placed their hands over their chest as a show of respect for Elice's words. She caught the eyes of her parents, who stared at her with their mouths parted. Then she looked at James, who wore a soft smile.

Her father engaged Lord Gref in conversation, while her mother spoke with Lady Gref. Elice used this opportunity to give a quick curtsey and mutter an "excuse me," then stepped away with James.

They didn't get more than a few feet before another couple greeted them. "Your Highness, my lord," a middle-aged gentleman said as he and the woman next to him bowed.

She curtseyed as James lowered his head in a show of respect. "Sir Phillip, Miss Irene," he greeted them and introduced Elice. She noted their names—Phillip, a soldier, and Irene, a prominent socialite. Elice knew she had to maintain proper etiquette with them if she wanted this night to go well. She made small talk, and James only added a few statements when needed.

After a short time, they excused themselves from this couple, only to be bombarded by another group—this time, a family with two young children. It carried on this way with group after group until Elice's throat went dry from a combination of all the nerves and the talking.

"Do you need something to drink?" James asked as they turned away from another guest.

"Please," she responded with a heavy voice, causing him to chuckle. They weren't far from a beverage table, so it was easy to make their way through the crowd in this corner of the room.

James requested two glasses of water from the servant, who poured the clear liquid from a pitcher into two stemmed glasses full of ice. The water slid down her parched throat, providing instant relief. She didn't realize her eyes were closed until she snapped them open at James's laugh.

"I haven't had water in hours," she confessed with a shy smile. "I was too nervous."

"I'll get you another." He turned to the servant and requested two more glasses.

Elice scanned the crowd and picked out her sister on the opposite side of the room. She waved, and Alice gave a demure gesture in return. Elice shook her head at Alice's shyness—then rolled her eyes at herself, knowing she was just as nervous.

Andre appeared behind Alice with a glass of a dark liquid. Elice lowered her hand and spun around, not wanting to look at him and risk souring her mood. It still upset her that Andre interfered with James's letter.

When she turned, James stared with a quirked eyebrow. He glanced behind her and nodded his head in understanding. "Are you all right?" He passed her the glass of water.

She nodded, then took a sip to avoid answering.

"Would you like to dance?" He pointed to the dance floor, now packed full of people.

Elice shook her head. "The music is too fast. I wouldn't be able to keep up."

James laughed. "You'll be fine. Just remember to focus on the beat. Besides, I'll be there to help you out."

The corner of her mouth turned up as she took in his smile. She shrugged and gave a nod, then took his hand so he could guide her through the crowd.

They found some room near the center of the floor. James held one of her hands and placed his other on her waist as he counted out the quick beats for her to dance in time to. Elice could only just hear him over the noise, but she was grateful for his thoughtful effort. Soon she didn't need him to count, and they were moving along with the flow of the crowd.

After two songs, the music changed from an upbeat tempo to a slow and soft melody. Wondering why they changed the beat, Elice looked toward the violinists. She found Miss Tabitha standing beside them, and the woman winked before sauntering away, a satisfied aura about her body as she moved.

Around her, several groups left the dance floor until only couples, young and old, remained. The pairs moved at a steady pace—their bodies pressed close together as they swayed from side to side to the sound of the sensuous violin strings.

Elice brought her eyes to James, who stared at her with a serious expression that brought heat to her cheeks. By the look on his face, Elice felt his wonder, his unasked question: would she be comfortable if they danced to this slow song?

He stepped away and extended his hand to her. "May I have this dance?"

Her face flushed as a few people around them glanced their way. His smile was irresistible, causing her to smile along with him as she reached for his hand. He placed both of her hands on his shoulders and pulled her by the waist until she was close. The affectionate action made her take a sharp inhale and turn her head to hide her reaction.

One by one, the other couples stopped dancing. They formed a circle around her and James, and she became so enthralled by the moment she had to close her eyes and rest a cheek against his shoulder to avoid their stares. She focused on their flowing movements, the back-and-forth sway of their bodies as he held her in place. A deep inhale brought an earthy aroma to her nose, and she sighed in its comfort—his smell reminded her of the forest, of freshly fallen leaves in autumn.

The unexpected sound of applause broke her from her thoughts, and her eyes shot open. The music had ended, and the crowd of birthday guests clapped. Yet the only thing she could focus on was James—his deep brown eyes, warm smile, earthy scent, and muscular arms around her waist. When the applause concluded and a new, fast-paced song replaced the slow piece, she pulled out of his embrace on unstable legs.

"I think I need another drink," she murmured and tugged on his hands to signal her need for departure.

He nodded in agreement, and they walked off the dance floor. The refreshment table was in their line of sight when James collided with someone, causing the person's glass to fall and shatter on the floor.

"My apologies," James said over the clamor of the party. Elice and James looked to see who he bumped into and found an enraged Andre and a nervous Alice. Andre stood with his hands balled into fists, his jaw clenched and tight. Without a word, he shoved James, who bumped into someone behind him. A few onlookers voiced their annoyance.

Elice helped steady James and then turned a furious glare on Andre. "What is wrong with you?"

"It was an accident, Lord Copita," James said through clenched teeth.

Andre swayed on his feet, his eyes bleary and unfocused. "You know how to ruin everything, James. You stole the woman I was courting."

Elice felt as if he knocked the wind out of her. "What?" she yelled, unable to think of anything else to say in response.

"What are you talking about?" James looked from Elice to Andre, his face falling as a frown appeared.

"Rita," Andre slurred, unaware of the attention he drew.

"Who?" Elice and James asked at the same time. They shared a questioning look before returning their attention to Andre.

Andre staggered, clearly drunk and not of his right mind. "Rita was my first love, and you stole her from me. I was courting her, but she—like everyone else, apparently—preferred you."

James shook his head and rested his hands on his hips. "I never courted her. She was just trying to lure rich men into marrying her. She ended up married to Lord Brant, who's nearly twenty years her senior. I can't believe you've been upset with me for two years over something so stupid."

"You're a liar, James. You stabbed me in the back. Then you went on to the academy and forgot all about me. Everyone's always talking about Captain James Taylor, the best soldier in all the kingdom." Andre gave him another shove, but his strength wasn't in it as he nearly stumbled to the ground.

James flexed his fingers in an attempt to calm himself. "You don't want to do that again, Lord Copita."

Elice, worried that Andre was already past the point of reason and James was on his way there, took a step to stand beside them and tried to catch their attention. Even Alice tried to step between them.

"Just calm down, both of you," Elice said, hoping they would listen to her.

"Why don't we all take a step back," Alice offered lightly.

The men ignored the princesses' attempts at peace and stepped closer to each other until they stood nose to nose. The guests closest to the scene showed great interest in the conversation between the royal princesses and their escorts, many of them openly listening and staring.

When Andre raised his right fist, Elice, fearing an all-out fight, knew she had to stop their dispute. She placed her hands in between the feuding men and blasted them with wind. The force of it pushed them away from each other, separating them before Andre could land a blow.

To Elice's horror, she called on too much wind. The air around their immediate vicinity blew, and a few people shrieked as they felt the sudden shift in the air. About a dozen guests looked around in amazement, asking what happened and why it became so drafty.

Elice's heart raced, and her stomach felt as if it had fallen to her feet. How would she explain this to her guests? Worse, how would she explain this to her father?

Without a word, she turned and ran from the area, looking for a place to hide before anyone noticed that the wind had come from her.

Seventeen

T he chill of the night air helped calm Elice's frayed nerves as she paced on the outdoor balcony. It was the closest place she could find to hide, but it turned out to be the perfect choice for her to regain composure.

When the patio door opened, she heard the commotion of the party. She turned to the door to see James sliding through the opening.

"Princess," he began, his shoulders slumped and his eyes not quite meeting hers, "please forgive me. I lost my patience."

Elice continued her pacing. "You don't know how embarrassed I feel. Now everyone will know I'm a mage, and my father won't forgive me this time." She didn't want to think how upset he would be once he found out—she'd been hiding for several minutes now, so she could only imagine he already knew.

James reached for her arms and held her in place. "They're not mad. Your parents and Miss Tabitha actually helped to ease the situation."

Elice stared at him with wide eyes. "What do you mean? Miss Tabitha ... does she know?"

He lowered his arms and nodded. "I suspect she's been watching you closely all night. As soon as you left, she rushed over and started talking about a strange draft that entered the room from the windows and doors. Your parents came and tried to dispel the growing crowd, but I don't think any of the guests suspect anything."

Elice, who had been holding her breath throughout his explanation, released a long exhale. She took in a couple more breaths. "How's Alice? She must feel worse than I do." She imagined her sister being overwhelmed after that intense moment and the ensuing chaos.

James sighed and shook his head. "She tried to drag Andre to a nearby table, but he stormed off. I asked her if she needed anything, but she told me to just find you."

Her heart clenched at the thought of her sister being all alone in that big room. "I should go to her. She shouldn't be alone on her birthday."

"I'll take you to where I last saw her."

Together, they crept inside. Elice looked around, studying everyone's expressions as she passed. She noticed the stares from people as they talked behind their hands.

"Is it true?" she heard someone whisper to another.

"I didn't see it, but I felt the wind change," someone else said.

"I felt the whole room shake."

"Do you think that's why they forced her into hiding?"

James held tight to her hand as he guided her through the parting crowd. She tried to ignore the whispers as she went, but every word carried across the wind to reach her ears. Her first instinct was to avoid their gawking by fixing her gaze on the ground as she trailed behind James. Then she remembered Miss Tabitha's words.

The time had come for her to shine, so now she would shine as brightly as a raging fire.

A flame lit inside her, and she held her head high, her chin sticking out as she searched for her sister. It didn't matter if they stared or gossiped about her. Dancing the night away with her sister and James took precedence.

"She was right here," James said when they stopped in front of an empty table.

"Let's look around." Elice pulled on his hand as they searched the large ballroom.

After several minutes of walking through her party guests—the crowd seemed thinner since people headed toward the exit in packs, looking over their shoulder at her—they found Alice standing in a corner near an easel and various paint supplies. A young man with thick, puffy hair and a painter's apron stood next to Alice. Judging by the way Alice grinned at the painter and the fact that they couldn't take their eyes off each other, Elice put the pieces together right away.

"It seems she's doing all right," Elice said with a smirk. She caught James's eyes, and he raised an eyebrow, which caused her to laugh.

"Is that..." He let the question trail off.

Elice nodded and pulled him away from the area before her sister noticed them—if she even looked away from the handsome young artist she was so captivated by.

Elice looked around; the hall was more than half-empty. Her parents approached, dragging their feet a bit, yet holding their heads high. She opened her mouth to apologize for her outburst, but her mother made the first move.

Julice pulled her daughter in for a hug. "My darling, the king and I are turning in. But please, stay up as long as you like."

Edgar patted James on the back. "Just don't keep her up too late."

"But what about—" Elice began.

Edgar held up a hand. "Not tonight. We'll talk in the morning."

Her parents left, walking arm-in-arm and chatting as they went.

Movement caught her eye, and she turned in time to see the painter leave the ballroom with his easel under his arm. She scanned the hall for her sister, finding her alone in the same corner.

"I'm going to check on Alice," she told James. She patted his arm as he nodded.

Alice stood near the wall with her eyes roaming over the crowd.

"How are you doing?" Elice asked carefully, assuming her sister might still feel embarrassed by Andre's earlier behavior.

Alice shrugged and laced her fingers in front of her body. "I think I'm ready for bed now."

Elice nodded her head. "It's been a long day. After everything with Dre..."

"Don't worry. I'm sure we'll have a long talk about it tomorrow."

"Your night wasn't all bad. I saw you talking with the painter. Was that Donovan?"

Alice's lips curled into a shy smile. "That was Donovan. And by the looks of it, you had a great time with James."

Elice's cheeks flushed. "We get along. He's a really great friend."

Her sister nodded her head toward the tables, where James sat down with two others. "You should get back to him before those girls try to snatch him away."

Elice laughed but shook her head. "Are you going to bed? I'll walk with you."

Alice waved her hand and stepped away from the wall. "You continue enjoying the party. I can make my way back to my room on my own."

Elice bit her lip. She wanted to spend more time with her sister on their birthday. "Are you sure?"

Alice gave her arm a gentle squeeze. "I'm sure. This is your first ball, so you have to be the last one out of the room."

They walked to the center of the room, where they shared a quick hug and bid each other good night. Elice watched her sister go, ignoring the looks from the remaining guests.

When she reached the table where James sat, she heard the high-pitched giggles the two girls made as they spoke. They seemed to be about her age and were strikingly gorgeous, wearing low-cut, form-fitting dresses. Their hands waved around as they spoke, eager to get James's attention. James, in contrast, leaned back in his chair and avoided eye contact with them.

His entire demeanor changed when he saw Elice. He stood and walked to meet her, his face lighting up as if thankful to see her.

"My princess, have you met Lady Paula and Lady Tina?"

The young ladies stood and curtseyed, yet their eyes showed little warmth.

"It's an honor to finally meet you, Your Highness," one of them said. She wore a bright pink gown that showed off her marvelous curves, tapering off above her knees. Elice had never seen a dress so short before.

The other girl, wearing a similar dress in a deep red, eyed her friend and gave a sideways smirk. "Yes, we've been dying to meet the mysterious princess no one's ever heard about."

"Tell me," said the first one, and she took a step forward and lowered her voice, "is it true what they're saying about you?"

As the girl in the red dress snickered, James took hold of Elice's hand. "Would you like to dance, my princess?"

Elice jutted out her chin, though her blood boiled. "I would love to, Lord Talin."

James muttered an "excuse us," and they turned to the dance floor. The musical selections were once again slow, and only couples danced while larger groups gathered for conversations at the tables. Most of the couples seemed oblivious to their surroundings, which likely meant they hadn't yet heard about Elice's slipup.

As they danced, she gave a nod in the direction from which they came. "They seem nice," she said sarcastically.

He looked over his shoulder with a scowl, his eyebrows drawing close together. "They usually aren't. They're only after one thing: marriage to a rich lord."

Elice quirked an eyebrow. "Is that why they were talking to you?"

"Probably." He took a deep breath. "I'm sorry you're not having a good time tonight."

She slowed her dancing to give him a playful shove. "Are you joking? I'm having a great time. There were some hiccups, but I think it'll be all right in the end."

He chuckled before he pulled her a little closer and resumed their dance. "Fate always seems to be on your side."

She snorted, knowing Miss Tabitha would've scolded her for making such a noise, but she didn't care at the moment. James's arms around her waist were too distracting. "Fate sure has a funny way of showing it."

"This night could've been a lot worse, I suppose."

She hummed in agreement. "I wonder how tomorrow will go. I'm dreading the conversation with my dad." She sighed and relaxed into a more comfortable position, with her arms resting on James's shoulders. He softened his stance as well, and they fell into a gentle sway in time with the violins.

"I think you've softened him up," he said, speaking into her hair at the top of her head.

She inclined her head to give him a look. "I can only hope so."

The conversation flowed like a calm breeze. She found out James was an only child until his mother remarried a wealthy landowner a few years ago. He now had a little sister who was only five years old. Elice shared her love of books, which was the reason she loved spending so much time in the library. To her surprise, he told her about the library in his estate—not as large as the royal library, he said, but still packed with shelves of books.

After several songs, Miss Tabitha walked up to them. "I hate to interrupt, but the musicians are ready to leave." Elice noticed the tiniest of smirks on the woman's face.

Only a few guests remained, and the staff looked dead on their feet. Both Elice and James uttered an apology. Miss Tabitha waved it off and said she would announce the end of the party.

Elice and James headed for the ballroom doors, and the remaining guests followed suit. They found themselves in a comfortable silence as James walked her to the staircase leading to the east wing of the castle. At the foot of the stairs, they stopped and stared at each other for a long moment.

James squeezed her hand. "I had an amazing night."

Elice swallowed against the tightness in her throat. "I did too."

"Can I see you tomorrow? Preferably during daylight hours." He wore a soft smile, and she returned it with a laugh.

"Maybe for lunch?"

His smile grew as he nodded. "I can break for lunch at midday." He gave her hand his signature kiss, then he bowed and whispered, "Goodnight."

"Goodnight," she returned as she walked backwards up the first step, causing her to lose her footing. Cursing, she turned to watch where she was going, ignoring the chuckle he gave and the fluster she felt at her embarrassment. She made it to the top without looking back and rushed into her room. The nerves of the day didn't slow, and she took her time dressing for sleep, which only came after much tossing and turning.

Eighteen

A loud knocking woke Elice from her sleep. With a groan, she mumbled from under her pillow for the person to enter.

Her father's rich voice called to her from the foyer, and she pushed herself up, her eyes popping wide open.

Pulling her hair into a high bun to hide the mess of curls, she trudged to the sitting room. Both her parents waited for her as she entered, already dressed in their formal daytime attire.

"Now that we have you alone, we need to talk about last night," her father said, sitting in one of the brown wing-backed chairs, Julice sitting next to him on the matching two-cushioned sofa.

Elice dragged her feet toward them and sat next to her mother. "I ... can explain?"

Julice shook her head while Edgar huffed. Elice took her time explaining why she had used her powers, to the king's great displeasure. His lips stayed in a tight line the entire time she spoke about the two young lords' feud and how she found herself awkwardly in the middle of it.

Edgar stood from his seat and began pacing around the room. When Elice finished, she closed her mouth and willed herself to keep it that way before she said anything else to get in more trouble.

"What do we do, Edgar?" Julice asked him. She held one of Elice's hands in hers as she spoke. "The castle is already talking about Elice's powers. A witness will come forward with the truth, regardless of what we say. But I refuse to lose my daughter again. You must fix this."

Elice stared doe-eyed at her mother. Her heart swelled as Julice set her steady gaze on Edgar, telling him with her eyes that she meant business.

The king stopped pacing and stared at them. "There's only one thing for me to do." Then he resumed his pacing. "I'll issue an official announcement confirming Elice's mage status and my removal of the magic ban all at once."

Elice jumped to her feet. "Are you serious?"

Edgar halted, a small smile pulling at his lips. "Well, it's a dumb law, anyway, right?"

With another leap, she ran to her father and fell into his arms. Edgar pulled her in for a tight hug, kissing the top of her head. "I created this mess in the first place. It's about time I own up to my mistakes—first, by apologizing for sending you away. I'm so sorry I caused you so much pain, Elice."

The tears flowed down her cheeks as she buried her face into her father's white shirt. She thought about pulling away before she ruined it, but he didn't attempt to push her away, so she stayed put.

He held her that way until her body stopped shaking and her eyes dried up. When she looked into his eyes, he gave her a warm smile and a nod. "Since that's now settled, I have work to do. I should make the proclamation today before we face too much backlash."

When he left the room, Julice walked over and wrapped Elice in a hug. She set her head on Elice's shoulder. "I better go talk with Miss Tabitha. We know how well she does with gossip." After another squeeze, Julice pulled away and left Elice to get dressed.

Elice met Alice in her room, and there she told her sister about the king's announcement. Alice sat on the edge of her bed, biting her nails. "By the Fates! I can't believe it! Are you going to be a madam now?"

Elice scrunched her nose. "I don't think so, and I don't want to be. I don't even know the rules about becoming one. But now I'm completely free to learn and train, at least."

They went to the dining room and sat together for a quick breakfast before heading out to enjoy a walk to their secret garden. Summer had fully settled upon the kingdom now. The sun's heat engulfed them, causing beads of sweat to form on Elice's forehead as they passed onto the terrace. She noticed the stares and whispers from everyone they passed, but Elice ignored them, since she would soon be free of the ridiculous ban.

Alice went straight for her canvas and readied her paint supplies while Elice sat with a book under the shade of a tree. She tried to focus on the words, but her mind wandered to the looming deadline she faced. Lenore hadn't responded to the summons yet.

If Lenore didn't show by dinnertime tomorrow night, she would remind her father of their pact and how she had—for the most part—upheld her end of the bargain.

Footsteps crunching on dry leaves brought the girls' attention to the hidden entrance of their enclosure. Andre bent beneath the low branches and made his way to them. Elice turned to her sister, expecting to find Alice mirroring her expression of shock. How did Andre know about this garden? Instead, Alice looked indifferent, as if she expected Andre's arrival. He must have been here before, which meant he was the only person outside the royal family who knew of this space.

"Good morning," he exclaimed as he came bounding in. Elice set her face in a glare at his zealous mood. After several steps, he stopped. The grin slid off his face as neither girl said anything in response to him. He cleared his throat and swung his arms back-and-forth before he clasped them in front of his body. "Right, that was too much. Let me try again." He sucked in a breath. "I owe you both an apology."

Elice glanced sideways at Alice, whose expression remained stony. Perhaps this was Alice's version of an angry face, Elice mused.

Andre folded his hands behind his back and looked Alice in the eyes. "Alice, we've been friends since we were children. That doesn't mean I've always treated you with the respect you deserve. Last night, I was a complete fool. I embarrassed you on your birthday. It's time I finally treat you like my best friend and my betrothed. You have the right to tell me when I'm acting like an idiot and put me in my place whenever the occasion presents, which I'm sure will be quite frequently."

Alice gave him a tiny nod.

He took a deep breath before turning his reluctant eyes on Elice. He flinched at her open glare. "Elice, I ruined your first birthday ball. What's worse is that it was my fault you used your magic in such a public space. I know people are talking, and someone's bound to address it with the king. It's all my fault. I've been acting without thinking these last few days. I've already told you why, and I now know your feelings for me are unrequited. I should never have let my feelings get in the way of your happiness."

When he finished his apology, Elice continued to shoot fireballs from her eyes at him. She wanted to accept his apology, yet she didn't know if she could fully believe him. His actions proved she couldn't trust his words.

Andre swung his arms by his side again. "All right, I'll let you princesses continue with what you were doing." He took a step back, his eyes darting back and forth between them, before turning and leaving the way he came.

Elice huffed and shook her head. "I really don't know how you deal with him, Alice."

Alice shrugged, picking up her paint bottles and adding more paint to her palette. "Andre's ridiculous sometimes, and he doesn't think before he acts. But he never meant to hurt either of us. I imagine he's learned his lesson. Having said that, I'm going to make him suffer a bit, just to make sure the lesson sticks."

They shared a secretive smirk before they returned to their tasks. Elice guessed her sister's idea of suffering would be supply runs to the art store, where Andre sat watch while Alice chatted with the cute shop owner.

∿

In the afternoon, Elice sat under the same oak tree, this time with James, enjoying a light lunch of her new favorite foods. She had gone into the kitchens—which shocked the staff since they usually didn't see royalty in their domain—and asked the cook for help in making meat and cheese sandwiches. Elice had never had fresh, thinly sliced portions of meat and cheese before she lived in the castle, so she gobbled them up every day since the first time Alice introduced them to her. Her other favorites were fresh fruit and lemonade, which made James chuckle when she told him how fond of them she was.

"What's so funny?" she asked, eyeing him over the rim of her clear glass. The ice inside started to melt, and the outside of the glass had a layer of cool condensation that felt good to hold on to in the sweltering summer heat.

He swallowed the last of his drink and peered into the empty glass. "You just reminded me how nice it is to enjoy the simple things. I forget to take things slow, to sit back and enjoy the things that once made me smile. Like ham and cheese sandwiches and a cool glass of lemonade."

"I might need to talk to my father about feeding the soldiers better food," she joked, which earned her another laugh. She set her face into a tight expression. "I have to tell you about what happened this morning with my father."

James finished chewing his strawberry as he waited, his hand slowly lowering to his lap in anticipation.

Elice held her breath, drawing out the moment before she exploded. "He's going to remove the ban!"

James's mouth fell open. "That's ... that's wonderful, Elice!"

She couldn't help the laugh she gave. She had never felt so euphoric in all her life. Reaching for another piece of fruit, she took a tiny bite, finding that she wanted another taste even though she couldn't eat anymore. "Would you like to have dinner with us tomorrow night?"

His eyebrows raised, and he coughed, almost choking on his food. "Of course. I'd be honored."

He could only spend thirty minutes on his break before he needed to return to his squadron. When they finished their lunch, they took their time packing up before leaving through the concealed entrance of branches.

A maid greeted her upon her arrival inside the castle. She curtseyed and handed Elice a note, which said her father requested her immediate presence in the throne room.

Her heart stopped, and a chill ran down her arms. Would he give the announcement already?

Lifting the skirt of her dress, she hurried through the halls, her long hair swaying behind her as she ran. She avoided bumping into people that were in the hall. She caught the words "magic" and "powers," but she didn't care what they thought anymore. Soon, she would be a free mage.

"I'm here," she said, panting and gasping for air the moment she burst through the throne room's massive double doors. Then she froze, losing all the air she had just collected in her lungs.

About sixty heads turned toward her, the shocked faces of men and women staring back at her own surprised expression. "Hello," she mumbled and gave a short wave.

"Princess Elice," Edgar bellowed from his throne at the other end of the hall. Julice sat in a matching seat next to his, and Alice stood to their father's left, her hands clasped in front of her. "Please, join us."

Elice tucked a loose curl behind her ear and tiptoed up to her father. "I'm sorry," she mouthed as soon as she approached, but he gave an imperceptible shake of his head and motioned for her to stand next to Alice.

Edgar set his hands to rest on the arms of his chair and addressed the group before him. "I have summoned you all here today for a special proclamation and announcement. My lords and ladies, take note that from this day forward, magic will no longer be banned from our kingdom."

The people in the room turned to one another, their eyes full as they whispered.

The king held up a hand, and the room fell silent once more. "Any and all mages who have been accused or convicted of breaking the previous ban are now absolved, and those who have already faced punishment are posthumously exonerated. Letters and compensation will be sent to the families of mages who have lost their loved ones due to this old law."

The room grew loud again as the lords and ladies of various lands talked over one another.

When the king stood, everyone snapped their mouths closed. They held their breaths, wondering what else he had to announce.

"As you may have heard, my youngest daughter, Her Royal Highness Princess Elice, has returned to live in the castle. It is my joy to announce that she is a mage. She spent her youth training under the tutelage of another and is now ready to join us in society."

If he had anything else to add, it was cut short when the questions poured in from those gathered in the room.

"What powers does she have, my king?"

"Does Princess Alice have powers as well?"

"Are you a mage, too, Your Highness?"

"What about the Fire Lords? Surely we should worry about them coming back?"

King Edgar raised his hands. "Enough." The nobility shut their mouths as the king drew in a deep breath. "You will write to your respective lands and share this news with the people. That is all."

One by one, the court filed out of the throne room, each member sparing an extra glance in the royal family's direction. With every glare, Elice stood a little straighter.

James stood at the back of the room and gave her a reassuring nod. He then walked out as quietly as he came, and soon the room had emptied of everyone except for a few guards.

Edgar dropped into his seat once the doors closed behind the last member of the court. Julice, still seated, rubbed a hand underneath her eyes as she sighed. Elice turned to her sister, and the two shared a shrug.

"Is that it, then?" Elice asked, eyeing her father as he hunched in his chair.

Edgar shook his head. "It's only begun, my dear child."

"Well, no one gave you a hard time. It seems as if all is well."

Her father stared up at the ceiling, and her mother reached over to pat his arm.

Alice leaned over to whisper in Elice's ear. "He means the nobility will probably push back against his ruling. Especially the more … how should I say it? Those who fear magic the most will try to get people on their side to stop the removal of the ban."

"Why would they do that? What do they have to fear?" Elice's voice rose with every word she spoke.

Edgar withdrew from his trance and stood up. "There is much to fear, I'm afraid. I'll need to prepare the troops." With that, he started for the door.

"The troops?" Elice called after her father, but he continued walking, and two guards flanked him as he left. She turned to her mother. "I don't get it. What's going on?"

Julice pushed herself up. "Once the news spreads, we will need to be ready for any uprisings. From the regular, or non-mage, citizenry, as well as from the mages. There are those who still believe in Orser's way of thinking."

Elice's eyes widened. "You mean the Fire Lords? They still exist?"

"Perhaps you can sit in on a council meeting one day." Julice gave a tight smile before she turned and walked out of the room, followed by another guard.

"I can't believe it," Elice mumbled as she looked around the room. Only two guards remained now. She wondered if her father assigned them to watch over her and her sister since he seemed so worried.

Alice breathed an audible breath. "The Fire Lords didn't die out with Orser. They simply went underground, hiding from Father and his ban. Now, they'll be able to come above ground."

Elice shook her head. "It's all my fault. Why didn't Father tell me? It would've been better to keep my powers secret until we were ready for this."

"I don't think there would've been a better time. We still have the upper hand. We have some time to prepare the soldiers and towns against any signs of trouble."

Elice wrung her hands. "Do you think it'll be just like before? Will the Fire Lords try to take over the kingdom?"

"Well, they don't have a leader anymore, right? They might cause some petty problems in the outer cities, but I doubt they'll try to come anywhere close to the capital." Alice pursed her lips, and a slight frown appeared on her face.

Elice followed her sister out of the throne room, looking back at the two guards that followed close behind.

Nineteen

The evening and following morning passed with Elice following the same routine as before, this time with her assigned security guard. Elice knew her father stayed in his council room until the middle of the night and awoke after only a few hours' rest. Her mother seemed worried, and she wore a frown or thin smile for most of the day.

Elice tried to spend her time reading, yet she couldn't focus on the pages of her book. It wasn't until everyone gathered for dinner—the usual company in their usual spots, with James taking the seat on Elice's left and next to Julice—that Elice questioned her decision about inviting James to dinner.

No one spoke a word throughout the first round of appetizers. The only sound came from the noise of forks clattering against the porcelain plates and the occasional harsh cough from Andre. Elice caught her sister's many glares aimed at him whenever he made a noise, though he tried his best to ignore it by looking down at his plate.

Edgar seemed oblivious to the agonizing silence, which struck Elice as odd, since he hated awkward silences as much as she did. Her father munched on his food as if he hadn't eaten anything all day. Since he didn't leave his meeting room, he likely hadn't eaten since breakfast.

"What did you accomplish today, Alice?" Edgar asked in between bites of his dessert.

Alice dug her fork into her piece of chocolate cake, but she only pushed the food around on her plate. "Oh, well, Andre and I spent the afternoon in town. I needed a few more art supplies." She gave Elice a shy smile before she continued. "When I returned, I looked over the drafts you gave me concerning the new boundaries for the fishing villages. Perhaps we can go over my proposed changes tomorrow?"

Edgar nodded in approval while Julice congratulated her for being so productive. Her mother then turned to Elice and asked, "What about you, dear?"

Elice swallowed a bite of her cake with a large gulp. "I read outside in the garden. Then I read inside the library. I had lunch with James in the garden, read some more in the library, then came here for dinner."

James cleared his throat while everyone else remained silent. Perhaps she really needed to find a hobby.

Elice used this opportunity to bring up the subject she had been thinking about all day. "This is a good point in time to bring up the fact that Lenore didn't show up, and the deadline was last night. I will remind you how I kept up my end of the deal."

Edgar took a draught of his wine before speaking. "It seems you are right. Though, I had a feeling it would work out this way and she wouldn't show."

"You remember the last part of the deal, right, Father? You would send your best man to find her."

"As promised, I will send my best man."

"Great," Elice said, placing her fork on the table. "I'll need a few supplies before I go. I can have a list ready in the morning."

King Edgar choked on his wine—everyone else around the table stared at Elice as if she spewed fireballs from her hands. "What do you need supplies for?" her father said with laughter.

"I'll need them for when I begin my search for Lenore." Elice didn't let her eye contact waver.

All laughter left Edgar's voice. "I've already promised to send my best soldier for the job. I will not be sending you."

"You said 'best man' for the job. Since Lenore is a mage, and none of your men are mages, clearly I will be the best person for this job."

"I will not be sending you out of the castle to search for Lenore." Edgar's voice rose as he placed his glass on the table.

Elice sat straight in her chair. "I'm the only one in this entire castle capable of finding her."

"Not after everything that's happened recently. It's too dangerous. I don't want you to get hurt."

"Nothing has changed, then. I'm still a prisoner here." Heat rushed to her face, and she clenched her hands into fists. Air blew around her, whipping her hair in various directions. The ground beneath her feet shook as the dirt under the marble floors threatened to rise.

James interrupted before she exploded. "If I may, my king. Perhaps I could go with her."

With his fists balled, Edgar brought them down on the table, causing his glass to shake. "I said no, and that's my last word on the matter."

Elice pushed herself out of the chair and stormed out of the room, a thick fog forming above her head as she stomped away.

She almost reached the east wing staircase when James called out to her. He reached for her arm to slow her down, but took a step back when water droplets fell from above. He looked up in wonder as more drops fell on his face. Meeting Elice's eyes, he closed the distance and wrapped her in a hug. "Your father's just stressed. The council's been tough on him, and I'm sure he's worried about what would happen if you left again."

She could feel the tension drain away, and the water around her dissipated. "I can't wait around anymore," she whispered, leaning into his shoulder. "I've wasted so much time and got sidetracked from what I should've done from the beginning. I need to find Lenore. With the magic ban removed and my father worried about the Fire Lords, I need answers now more than ever."

James nodded, but wore a thin expression when he looked down at her. "Are you going to leave tonight?"

"I have to," she answered.

"I was serious when I said I'd go with you."

Elice shook her head and pulled out of his embrace. "You should stay. I don't know how long I'll be gone, and you have duties here as a captain. My father's going to need you. Besides, I'm a mage. I can take care of myself."

James stepped forward again and grasped her hand. "I know you can take care of yourself. That's not what I'm worried about. I just want to make sure you come back."

Elice's breath caught as he raised a hand to her cheek. He brushed her curls to the side, and with his knuckles, caressed her flushed skin. "Will you promise to come back?" he whispered, his eyes staring deep into hers.

She couldn't move her head to nod—couldn't open her mouth to say that she would return. She stood there with her eyes boring into his. The echo of footsteps broke their enchanted gaze. Elice squeezed the hand that held hers to relay her message, and as she backed away, their fingers slowly slid apart.

When she couldn't hold on to his gaze any longer, she forced her eyes away, hoping he understood her feelings by the look in her eyes—even if she didn't understand them herself.

~

With a few clothes and a canteen of water packed in a small shoulder bag, the only thing Elice had left to do was wait until midnight when the east tower guard fell asleep. At ten minutes until midnight, she planned to creep out of her room, hoping no one would catch her in her escape.

She paced her bedroom floor as the minutes ticked by. Only the Fates were on her side, guiding her down this path she knew would be wrought with unknowns. With a sudden realization, she turned toward her vanity and grabbed Lenore's necklace. At least she could have one familiar thing with her. She threw it into the bag, then resumed her pacing.

The bedchamber's outer door creaked open, and she froze in place, clutching the bag behind her back. She waited, hearing muffled voices on the other side of her bedroom door until it slid open.

A single candle lit the room, but she could see Alice and Andre as they made their way inside. They each had a bag over their shoulders.

"What are you doing here?" she asked as Andre closed the door behind them.

Alice stepped forward to answer in a whisper. "James told us you're planning on leaving to find Madam Lenore."

"I have to." Elice lifted her chin, ready for their challenge. She wouldn't let them talk her out of leaving this time.

"Not without us," Andre said, stepping forward to stand level with Alice.

Elice shook her head. That was why they had bags, were dressed in loose traveling clothes, and wore thick rubber-soled shoes. "You can't come with me. I don't know how long it'll take, and Lenore has proven to be untrustworthy."

"We can't let you go by yourself," Andre countered and then held up his bag. "We've packed supplies, dried meats and fruit, and a small medical kit."

Elice shook her head again, not wanting to accept their help because she was too afraid of what might happen. "If anything happens to you..."

Alice closed the distance and grabbed both her hands. "That's why we need to come with you. If anything should happen to you, I would never forgive myself. I finally have you in my life, and I will not let you do this—do anything important—on your own. Besides, a great and powerful person once told me that breaking the rules is all right if the rules are wrong."

With tears brimming her eyes, Elice huffed a laugh. "That's not exactly what I said, but you're on the right path, I suppose."

Andre and Alice stared at her, their eyes as steady with determination as her own. She looked at the silver clock that sat on her vanity. Both hands pointed at twelve—she needed to leave now before anyone else caught her.

Elice nodded despite herself. She knew she needed help, and Andre knew the Jani Forest better than she did. "We'll check the cabin first. If she's not there, I can leave her a note and then move on to check the other towns to the east of the forest."

Andre threw his bag over his shoulder. "From there, we can head south toward Fort Brant. The nomads have a trading outpost near the fishing villages, and they've long been suspected of continuing to use magic. We might find someone there who has information."

With a small plan hatched out, they left the room and headed for the east tower. Just as before, the guard slept on as they snuck out undetected. Elice imagined James looking out toward the tower, hoping to catch a glimpse of her as she left.

In the first hour of their travel into the dark night, they kept a whispered conversation. Andre detailed the path from the castle to the cabin in the middle of the vast forest. He admitted he found it by accident the first time, and this time the group would have to travel in complete darkness. He assured them that he was an excellent tracker, which was how he was able to find Elice's cottage in the first place.

"The way to Fort Brant is easier," he said. "If Madam Lenore isn't at the cottage, we should rest there for a few hours and take off in the morning."

The two girls agreed as they ducked under a branch that Andre lifted for them. They followed his lead, Elice taking up the middle position and Alice bringing up the rear. They couldn't see their feet, and Elice slipped more than once on overgrown tree roots.

Another hour passed, and it felt as if they weren't making any progress at all. They moved at a snail's pace, watching each step with care. Alice trailed off further behind than Elice liked, and she and Andre called to her every so often to check on her.

Suddenly Alice shrieked, and the sound of a body thudding to the ground followed. Elice turned and ran to find her sister, with Andre coming up right behind her.

"Alice," she yelled, seeing her lying on her stomach in the dry dirt.

"I'm fine," Alice said with a grimace as she rolled herself over. She cried in pain and grasped at her ankle, bringing her knee to her chest. "I think I tripped on a root."

Andre kneeled beside her. He touched her ankle, and she hissed in pain. Gently, he rolled it around, and Alice dug her fingernails into her knee. "I don't think it's broken, just sprained," he said after a moment. "We should make camp here and take off at morning's first light."

Elice bit her lip, wanting to protest, but she knew by looking at her sister that they couldn't continue like this.

Andre grabbed his bag and looked through it. He pulled out a thick white cloth and began wrapping Alice's ankle. She hissed at the pressure on her injured ankle, and tears formed in her eyes. A thin layer of dirt now collected on her clothes from the fall, and Elice wondered if her sister had ever looked this worse-for-wear.

Elice grabbed a thin blanket from her bag and kneeled beside Alice. With the blanket folded, she placed it under her sister's bandaged ankle.

"I'm sorry for being so clumsy," Alice muttered through clenched teeth.

Elice patted her shoulder. "It's fine."

She and Andre worked to set them up for the remaining hours of the night. They ate a bit from the rations they had brought with them, knowing they could buy more food at the eastern fort with the gold coins Andre packed. Since it was a warm summer night, they didn't need to light a fire or wrap themselves in heavy blankets.

"I'll stay up to watch for any wild animals or weary travelers looking to loot from us," Andre said as he plopped down on the hard floor.

Elice waved him off. "No, I'll do it. I'm still buzzing from the adrenaline of it all. I couldn't sleep even if I tried."

Andre gave her a side-eyed glance, but nodded anyway.

After several long minutes, Elice heard their light snores. As she leaned against a tree, her bag on the ground next to her legs, she thought about what she had to do. She clutched at the straps of her bag and sent a silent prayer to the Fates, hoping she was making the right choice.

Elice whispered an apology as she stood and crept away from their makeshift camp. In her mind, she told herself she had wasted so much time already. Now, with Alice injured, the trip to the cottage became that much harder. Not to mention the long journey afterward in case Lenore wasn't even at the cottage.

They would only slow me down, she reasoned with herself, as she made her way through the thick trees. Thanks to Andre, she already had a vague idea of where to go. With this being her second trip through the forest, she figured she would be able to find her way.

About an hour later, she found the edge of the forest that led to the familiar clearing she grew up in. Her heart clenched as she crept closer to the cottage she knew, hidden in the shadows of tall trees and the dark night. She guessed it to be around four in the morning, still too early for the sun to rise. If Lenore was home, she didn't want to alert the woman of her presence by scaring her.

Elice walked to the front door and eased it open. It made the faintest of sounds as the old hinges croaked. "Lenore?" she called out into the dark room. She remained still, listening for the old woman. She heard nothing, not even the sound of the woman's heavy breathing.

Still, Elice had to check the bedroom in case the old mage slept through Elice's call. "Lenore, are you home?" she tried again, this time louder.

It remained silent as she made her way to the bedroom door. Elice raised her hand to knock, but it squeaked as it shifted ajar. She pushed it all the way open and walked through.

As she stepped inside, she opened her mouth to call out Lenore's name once more. Instead, she felt a sharp pain on the side of her head. Her vision blurred as she dropped to her knees. She lifted a hand, but before she could touch her throbbing temple, she lost consciousness as she fell to the floor.

Twenty

A bright light shined through her closed eyes, forcing her awake. She squinted to avoid the uncomfortable feeling of the blinding light. Elice blinked until her eyes adjusted to the sudden change in brightness. She attempted to sit up but felt a stinging pain near her left eye. Groaning, she touched the spot and felt a sticky substance. She looked at her fingers, which were coated in blood.

She remembered leaving Andre and Alice asleep in the middle of the forest and finding her way to the cottage. Then she remembered walking into what she thought was an empty house. Grimacing at the pain in her head, she recalled being hit and falling unconscious.

Looking around, she lay in the middle of Lenore's bedroom. A few steps away, she saw a jagged rock bigger than her hand, also spotted with blood. With another groan, she pushed herself to a sitting position and then took a steadying breath before attempting to stand.

Her legs wobbled as she stood, but she resolved herself enough to leave the room. Whoever had attacked her might still be out there—she had to find Alice and Andre before her attacker found them first.

She stumbled her way out of the tiny house and into the warm morning sun. It took her eyes a moment to become accustomed to the change in light, which also made her aching head throb.

When she regained focus, she saw Alice and Andre in front of her. Her breath caught as she took in their current state: both sat on the ground, their wrists bound by rope and their mouths gagged by a thin cloth. She took a step toward them, but stopped when she heard a familiar croaky voice.

"I see you're awake," Lenore muttered, her voice thick. Elice turned her head toward the sound, causing her head to throb once more at the sudden movement. "I was beginning to think he hit you too hard."

Lenore stood off to the side near the outer wall of the house, wearing a long purple cloak that reached the floor. A lanky man with a large beard and even longer hair stood next to her. His red robe angled halfway off his shoulders, and he leaned against the wall with his arms crossed.

Elice took in the scene before her, trying to make sense of it. Lenore read from her spell journal, not even bothering to spare Elice a glance. The man, however, bore his rounded eyes on Elice with a sly smirk on his lips. He pushed his thick, matted hair out of his face as he continued to stare. Elice knew this man was a fire mage just by looking at him. She could almost feel the heat radiating off his skin.

Her heart pounded deep in her chest as she wondered what spell Lenore could be reading, since she was only a sight mage and didn't have any other powers. Then she realized Lenore had the chain of her necklace wrapped around her palm. The woman must have taken it from Elice's bag when she was knocked out. What spell could she possibly use with that necklace? *It's a protection charm after all*, Elice thought.

Taking a breath, she took a hesitant step toward the old woman and the burly fire mage. "Lenore, what's going on?"

The old mage kept her focus on the notebook. "The ritual has begun."

Elice swallowed and caught her sister's eye, which wandered between her and Lenore, unsure where to keep her attention. When she looked at Andre, he had his eyes set on her and he shook his head, trying to tell her something she didn't understand.

She returned her gaze to Lenore. "What ritual?"

Lenore looked up from her book. "The one that will bring Orser back." Her coarse voice made the hairs on Elice's arms stand up.

Elice looked back at Alice and Andre, sure that her wide eyes matched theirs. The stranger in the red coat shifted his weight, bringing Elice's attention back to him and the old woman. "Please, Lenore, just let them go. You and I can talk by ourselves. You don't need them here."

The woman chuckled, but the sound turned into a rough cough.

The man patted her on the back, but she smacked his hand away.

"All we need is one sacrifice," he said with a sneer.

Elice shook her head, not wanting to believe what she heard. "You don't need to do this, Lenore. The ban has been lifted. We're free to practice magic again."

"You stupid girl," Lenore spat. "This is exactly what I've been working toward all these years."

Elice's cheeks flushed. "Is that why you stole me from my parents, why you stole my childhood? All to bring back some murdering lunatic?"

Lenore's cloudy gray eyes darkened. "I saw this moment long ago."

"You mean the vision you lied to my parents about?" Elice crossed her arms over her chest. "I know all about that. How you took advantage of their fear of mages with some lie about my powers to take me away from them."

Lenore waved a hand at her and spoke with a slow, tired voice. "Not that vision. The one I had when I first met Orser. This is what I saw. I've been working by the Fates' design to make that vision come true. I even betrayed Orser by helping your father destroy the Blood Flower. Everything I've done has led to this moment. I can bring him back from the dead to face off against his greatest threat. You are the only one strong enough to fight against him. And when he defeats you, no one will dare challenge him again."

Elice's body froze as if she had slipped into an icy pond and couldn't escape. "This is madness," she muttered, shaking her head. "I won't let you kill my sister or Andre."

Lenore scoffed. "Why would you protect them? They aren't like you." Lenore used her walking cane and hobbled closer to Elice.

"You could join me, you know. Together we can bring Orser back. Together, we can fight by his side to bring down the system that hates people like us. I raised you, watched over you. I knew you practiced when I wasn't looking, growing stronger every day. With your power, you can help us. You can be the greatest ally in this war against non-mages."

It was Elice who scoffed this time. "I would never fight with Orser. We should work together—mages and non-mages. There doesn't need to be another war."

"Why should I care about those people when they only try to hurt people like me? My family abandoned me when I was just fourteen. Orser's own parents tried to kill him because he was born a fire mage. All over this pathetic kingdom, mages are discriminated against for simply being born different. Fire mages have it worse than all of us. People view them as destructive and toxic. But it's not their fault their powers manifest that way. The only way to make it better is by fighting and getting rid of those who call themselves in charge." Lenore panted at the end of her speech, leaning heavily on her cane.

Elice shook her head. "Nothing can excuse what Orser and the Fire Lords have done. The only way to make things better is by showing people we aren't bad. Doing this will only make them fear us more. But we can change that if we do what's right."

"You're a fool," Lenore said, the corner of her lip turning up. "People never do what's right for everyone else, only what's right for themselves. Alas, it doesn't matter now. Orser will soon return to finish what we started."

"I'm begging you, Lenore. Don't do this," Elice implored. She took a step closer to Lenore, angling her body so she blocked the woman's path to her sister and Andre. She drew in a deep breath. "If you don't stop ... I'll have to stop you myself."

Lenore gave a dry chuckle. "You would never hurt me."

With a grunt, Lenore's companion pushed himself off the wall. "I'll take care of this, Madam Lenore." He opened his hands and two balls of swirling fire appeared. Both of his palms became engulfed in flame as he held them in front of his body.

Elice gulped but raised her hands, calling on the elements. Air and water molecules came rushing to her hand, and a cyclone about two feet tall formed in her palm. Wind blew all around them, and the dirt from the ground lifted into the storm. She stumbled and almost lost control when she realized she finally incorporated earth magic into this spell.

Lenore squinted at Elice through the spiraling winds. "I see you've been practicing new tricks."

"Stop the ritual. Now." Elice's voice shook with the force of having to raise it over the sound of the rushing wind. She hoped Lenore and the fire mage didn't hear the wobble in her voice and would just back down due to the size of her spell. She really didn't want to hurt the old woman who had raised her.

The man's flames spiked and flared as he stepped forward and threw a fireball toward her. Elice dodged it as best as she could, but her focus remained more on her storm than the incoming attack. It flew straight at her feet, and she couldn't jump back enough to avoid it. The flames bit at her shoes and ignited the legs of her pants before she used the moisture from her storm to put it out.

Her legs trembled as the burns made her ankles swell in pain, and a cry escaped her mouth. She forced herself to stand tall, though, as the fire mage readied another fireball.

Elice took in a deep breath, and on the exhalation, she forced the cyclone toward him. She almost tripped as it flew from her hand. It knocked him on his back a few feet away, his head bouncing on the ground. His fire magic faded as he fell, and he didn't stir after he landed.

Elice used this opportunity to hobble toward her sister, who sat in the grass with her legs outstretched. Her ankles burned with each step she took.

She threw herself at her sister's feet and pulled the gag over Alice's head. "Are you hurt?" she asked, working to remove the rope around her wrists. Alice shook her head, but Elice remembered her bandaged ankle from a few hours ago. "Can you walk?"

"I don't know—I ... I think so," Alice stammered.

Elice nodded and ran to Andre, removing his gag and loosening his ties. "How about you? Are you all right?"

"I'm fine, I'm fine," he said, helping her pull the rope off.

Elice gripped his wrists and held his gaze. "You need to get Alice out of here. I don't think she can walk."

"I'm not leaving you," he told her, his voice firm.

"You have to. I shouldn't have let you two come. I knew it was dangerous. The Fates tried to warn me all night. Now they're punishing me by hurting you and Alice."

"If you get hurt—"

"I'll be fine." Elice stood and extended her hand for Andre, helping to pull him up. She held back the grimace from her face when the pain shot up her burned legs. He opened his mouth to say something, but snapped it shut as his eyes narrowed, focusing on something behind Elice's shoulder.

Elice whipped around. Lenore stood directly behind Alice with a sharp knife in her hand, pointing it at the side of her sister's neck. The necklace dangled at the end of Lenore's hand, shaking as her hand wobbled. Lenore must have been too slow even with her walking cane because she stood a couple of feet away, the knife hovering a few inches away from Alice's neck.

"This is not over yet, girl," Lenore rasped, out of breath.

Elice stepped forward, and Lenore matched her motion with a limp toward Alice. Alice gasped as the point of the blade met her neck, and her hands flew to her mouth, muting her shriek.

"Stop!" Elice clenched her fists, painfully aware that Lenore had challenged her to choose. She did not want to hurt Lenore, but she would *not* let Lenore hurt Alice. She tried to reason with her one last time. "Drop the knife, or I'll have to make you." A tear ran down her cheek as she looked at the woman she was forced to grow up with, threatening the life of someone she needed in her life all along. "Don't make me do this."

"Our fates have already been decided, girl," Lenore said, still panting for air.

As Lenore closed the distance, Elice set her jaw and called to the wind.

With as much power as she could muster, she drew on a large gust and forced it in their direction. She spread out her arms in front of her body as she guided the air straight at Lenore. She kept her eyes open long enough to see the knife pierce Alice's skin before it flew backward in Lenore's grip due to the strong wind current.

At the same time, the force blew Alice and Lenore to the ground.

When the last of Elice's energy faded away, she dropped her arms and fell to her hands and knees, her legs finally giving up on her.

Andre rushed to Alice's side and called out to her. "Are you hurt? Alice, talk to me."

Elice pushed on the ground and stood on weak legs, stumbling closer to see Alice lying unconscious on the floor. She stepped away and staggered to Lenore's body. A sinking weight pulled at her chest as she saw the protection charm in the dirt, and the knife plunged deep into the old woman's chest.

She clamped her hand over her mouth, and she sank to her knees once more. Blood seeped from the wound, soaking through the cotton shirt on Lenore's motionless body.

Elice reached out a shaky hand and shook Lenore's shoulder as if to jar her awake from a deep sleep. Tears streamed down her face as she threw her body on top of the lifeless form below her. With a shaky hand, she reached for the necklace and pulled it close, hugging it to her chest as she cried.

Time passed as if in a blur. Her body shook with sobs as she held on to the woman she had once cared for, the woman she had loved like a mother, even if the love was one-sided.

She realized someone was shaking her shoulders and calling her name. She didn't think to answer their call. After a few moments, a pair of muscular arms lifted her to her feet. On the way up, she glimpsed Lenore's blood-soaked body. Her stomach churned, yet she couldn't look away.

Someone called her name again. This time, the person gripped her chin and turned her head. Her eyes locked on James's frown.

In the back of her mind, she wondered why he was there. Her ears picked up the sound of several voices and of horses neighing. She looked behind James's shoulder to see soldiers on horseback approaching the field, some already off their horses and surveying the area. At the forefront stood King Edgar, barking orders at his soldiers.

Her mind only processed the new arrivals for a moment before she returned her teary gaze to Lenore.

James, still holding her by the chin, gently turned her face toward him again. "Hey. Look at me. You don't have to look at that anymore."

Elice swallowed, but her throat hurt from all of her wailing. She looked down at her hands, taking in the blood and the dirt soaking her body and dripping from the necklace. Her vision obscured as fresh tears tumbled down her face. The pain in her ankles flared, reminding her of the burns she received. She heard James's voice again, though she didn't know if he spoke to her or someone else. The last thing she noted was being pulled to a nearby horse.

~

Elice sat in the council room. She didn't remember the trip back to the castle or how she ended up in the chair she found herself in. Feeling a warm hand gripping hers, she followed the person's arm up to its owner's face. James sat next to her. He stared straight ahead with his brows knitted together. She snapped her eyes to her lap before he caught her staring. She realized she still held on to the necklace, and it was still caked in bloody dirt.

The door opened, but she didn't look to see who had entered. Instead, she heard her father's stern voice. "Has she said anything?"

James let go of her hand, sighing as he stood up. "No, my king. She must be in shock."

"And the prisoner?"

"Still unconscious."

Edgar moved closer to them and lowered his voice. "The blood?"

"Except for the gash on her head, it's all Madam Lenore's."

Reminded of the throbbing pain near her temple, she touched the spot and hissed out a breath when the pain worsened on contact.

James rushed to her side and pulled her hand away. "Try not to touch it, my princess. The doctor will stitch it up after he finishes checking on Princess Alice."

Her vision flashed with the image of her sister lying on the ground next to Lenore's body. "Alice. Where is she? Is she all right? I need to see her." She moved to stand but staggered around, her body weakened from the head injury and the trauma she sustained.

Her father steadied her by the shoulders. "I need to talk to you first. I need to hear from you what happened."

Elice nodded, regretting the movement when her head started pounding again. She recounted last night's events, from Andre and Alice approaching her to getting hit in the head by Lenore.

She touched the side of her head, and her lips trembled. "I tried to get her to stop. I begged her. But she wouldn't listen. I had to stop her. I had to." Slow-moving tears fell from her eyes at the realization. She killed Lenore. All she wanted to do was talk to her—to find out the truth about why she took her from her family.

Now, the woman lay dead, struck down by Elice's own hands.

Edgar squeezed her shoulders. "Can you confirm Lenore was going to kill Alice if you hadn't stopped her?"

She nodded, her tears still falling. "She had a knife to her neck. I had to protect Alice. I couldn't let her die."

Her father grabbed her hands and brought them to his chest. "Thank you for being so brave and for protecting your sister. I thank the Fates you both are safe." He pulled her into a hug, and Elice buried her face in his chest.

When she pulled away, he had tears in his eyes as well. He wiped her eyes, letting his tears well up and fall down his cheeks. "Let's go check on your sister." He grabbed her hand before calling to James. "You too, Captain."

James followed close behind them as they rushed straight into Alice's room. Inside, a doctor stood beside Alice while Julice and Andre stood by the foot of the bed. Elice rushed past everyone and kneeled beside Alice's unconscious body.

"Why is she still not awake?" Elice asked. She threw the filthy chain around her neck before she grabbed her sister's motionless hand.

The doctor sighed and grabbed his bag. "She was awake moments ago. I had to give her something to stop the hysteria."

Elice looked at him with furrowed eyebrows. "What do you mean?"

Andre answered for the doctor. "She came to on the ride back to the castle. She was screaming the entire time, yelling nonsense."

"What did she say? What's wrong with her?"

He shook his head. "It was nothing, Elice."

The doctor cleared his throat. "She's just in shock. The medicine I prescribed should help her relax a little when she next wakes. Please, Princess Elice, I heard you have a head wound. I'll check it for you now."

She sat at the edge of the bed while the doctor examined her head, then stitched the gaping one-inch hole she didn't realize she had. After he checked and cleaned her burns, he packed up, leaving behind some healing salves for her.

Elice turned to Andre once the door closed behind the doctor. "What was Alice screaming about, Dre?"

"It's nothing, Elice." His face grew dark, and his eyes seemed to cloud over. Elice was reminded of the first time she saw this serious expression on his face, and she knew he was hiding something.

"Why won't you tell me? Was it that bad?"

Andre looked around the room, his lips in a thin line. "She kept yelling about some flower, saying 'it's going to bloom again.' Really, Elice, it's probably best if we let it go."

"Is that all she said?" She looked at her sister's face, the smears of dirt and dried blood on her neck blemishing her beautiful brown skin.

At Andre's hesitation, she looked at him again. He shifted his feet, avoiding her eyes. "She said, 'he's coming back.'"

Edgar huffed and placed a hand on his hip. "What in the Fates' name does that mean?"

"I think I know what Alice was screaming about." Elice gave Andre a look, but he shook his head. "It's like Lenore said."

"Orser is dead, Elice," Andre said. "Whatever Madam Lenore said was wrong—more lies."

"What's this?" Edgar asked, looking at her and Andre.

"Lenore was performing a ritual," Elice answered, now hesitant to go into that detail. "She was trying to ... bring Orser back."

"But she failed." Andre cut her off from saying anything more. "You stopped her from completing the ritual."

"What did she need for this ritual?" Julice asked.

Elice opened her mouth but snapped it shut. She met Andre's eyes, his wide with fear as he, too, realized the same thing.

They all looked between her and Andre, waiting for one of them to reply.

"Well," Edgar said with a wave of his hand, "what did she need?"

Elice swallowed, finding her mouth dry and raw, and she was only able to squeeze out three words. "A human sacrifice."

The words hung in the air like a thick fog, engulfing their bodies and stealing their breath.

Epilogue

Summer was winding down too quickly—the leaves of the trees were changing color and cool air drifted across Highmore from the northern mountains. Elice threw the front doors open, meeting the fresh breeze head-on as she stepped outside the castle's front door. Today was the day—her first day out of the castle without having to sneak. She couldn't help the waves that tumbled around in her stomach as she thought about it.

Alice stepped beside her, supported by Andre. Elice turned to her, the smile falling off her face.

"We don't have to go out today," she told Alice. "We can go another day when you're feeling better."

James came to stand by her other side. "Are you trying to postpone this trip to the village again?"

"I believe she is," Alice answered with the tiniest of smirks. "I've told you ten times today. I'm fine. The medicine the doctor gave me helps with the headaches. Besides, I haven't had one of those bad dreams in days."

Elice bit her lip. Alice had been having constant nightmares, even during daylight hours. Everyone grew worried, so they asked the doctor to prescribe her a stronger medicine. So far, the new prescription seemed to work, but Elice was still worried for her sister. Alice complained of headaches, and Elice couldn't get rid of the image of her sister's hysterical screams whenever she had a nightmare.

"Well," Elice began, "as soon as you're ready to go, we'll return to the palace."

"You're worrying too much, Elice," Andre cut in, rolling his eyes.

"Of course, she's worried," James said, crossing his arms. "After everything these two have been through—"

"What? You think I don't know what they've been through?"

Elice rolled her eyes as the two of them continued their bickering. Alice linked their arms and asked, "Are you ready?"

Looking past the open gates, she could see the beginning of the village and the shops she had yet to explore. She thought about what lay beyond the village, the many unknowns, and even more possibilities she wanted to discover.

With a nod, she took a deep breath and walked arm-in-arm with her sister toward the castle gates.

∿

The damp stone hallways glowed with a single lantern. A man

wearing a crimson cape walked down the corridor as it snaked its way deep underground. His footsteps echoed and splashed on the water-strewn floor until he came to a stop in front of a closed wooden door. He knocked and received an answer from within to enter.

The hooded figure pushed the door open, closing it behind him, and walked into the dim room. He continued until he stood before an older man. He wore an identical cape and sat on a creaky wooden chair.

He kneeled before his elder, withdrew a piece of paper from his robe, and handed it to him. "It is as she said. The time has come—we must prepare."

The elder nodded and grabbed the paper. He unfolded it with wrinkled fingers and looked at its contents.

It was the front page of a newspaper. The heading read, "Royal Representatives Confirm Rumors of Madam Lenore's Mysterious Death," with a portrait of Princess Elice, standing beside her family at the foot of the castle's promenade.

A sneer spread across the elderly man's face as he read the caption below. When he finished, he looked at the younger man and gave him a wave of his hand. "Go. Ready the others."

"Yes, Lord Victor," the young man nodded before he stood and left the room.

Lord Victor returned his gaze to the newspaper clipping and smirked.

Note from the Author

I hope you enjoyed reading the beginning of Elice's journey. Her story continues in book two, Tomb of Souls, available now.

If you enjoyed this book, please spread the love by leaving a review to help other readers find out about it!

WANT EXCLUSIVE BONUS CONTENT?

READ THE ALTERNATE FIRST CHAPTER, TOLD FROM ALICE'S POV.

DOWNLOAD IT FOR FREE AT WWW.JENNIFERROACHFORD.COM.

To be informed about future release dates or to sign up for my Advanced Reader Copy (ARC) list, sign up for my newsletter at www.jenniferroachford.com.

Are you ready to join my Army of Mages? Join my exclusive street team, where you'll get first access to my books, as well as swag and other fun giveaways. Visit Jennifer's Army of Mages Reader Group on Facebook to be part of the club.

Acknowledgements

I actually had a dream about Elice. She had thick, unruly curls and beautiful brown skin. After years of mulling, her story sprouted from my mind, shooting forth like the vines she so easily pulls from the ground. To tell her story is to share a little piece of me. I only wish I could send a blast of wind from my hands or control the weather with my emotions. Then again, maybe I'm the lucky one.

Thanks to all my amazing readers who helped me shape this story into what it is today. I used your encouragement to propel me further and build a better world. I'm so thankful to have had so much help along the way. I want to thank my Army of Mages for continuing to read my work and for being my biggest supporters.

To Aamna Shahid, MC Damon, and the entire team at Etheric Designs. You are all seriously amazing, and your work is spectacular.

To my family and friends: I appreciate all the support you've given me all my life, and for continuing to support me as I live out my dream.

To my husband and children: you are the reason I do this. You watched me stay up late into the night and struggle with the oddities of word placement and dangling modifiers. Words can't describe how much I love you for putting up with me as I share my books with the world.

About the Author

Jennifer Roachford is a wife, mom, and the author behind the **Elice, the Great** and **Lenora, the Cursed** trilogies—diverse fantasy worlds built for readers who have always wanted to see themselves in the pages of a book.

As an Afro-Latina, Jennifer believes representation isn't just important, it's essential. Her passion for storytelling was born from a lifelong love of books, and she channels that love into every character she creates and every world she builds.

When she isn't writing her next novel or editing someone else's manuscript, you can find her in the garden daydreaming about books or hunting down the perfect cup of coffee on snow days. She also bakes—because every great story deserves a good snack.

www.ingramcontent.com/pod-product-compliance
Lightning Source LLC
Chambersburg PA
CBHW060921190726
48286CB00002B/593